CW01091364

Other titles by Linda Hoy available in Armada

Nightmare Park

Ring of Death

Linda Hoy

Ring of Death was first published in Armada
in 1990

Armada is an imprint of the Children's Division, part of the
Collins Publishing Group,
8 Grafton Street, London W1X 3LA

Copyright © Linda Hoy 1990

Printed and bound in Great Britain by
William Collins Sons & Co. Ltd

Set in Times 11/12 pt.

A group of pupils from schools in Bury created the idea for this story when they worked together at Castle Head in the spring of 1988. Linda Hoy has supplemented and altered their ideas, but the original concept remains the same and she has them to thank for their inspiration.The setting of the book is real. Castle Head is a field studies centre, near Grange over Sands, which was built by John Wilkinson, the iron master, and the episode about him and his relationship with Anne Lewis is true. Cedric Robinson, the guide across the sands, is a real person as well, but all the other characters in the book are fictitious.

I would like to thank the following people who have helped with the writing of this book. First of all, the pupils from various schools in Bury:

Philip Dipnall, David Thomason, Elizabeth Ware, John Driver, Alan Jackson, Richard Smith, Simon Wood, Li Ping Yip, Vanessa Squires, Joanne Woods, Jenni Bardi, Lee Buckley, Denise McWilliam.

Secondly, the staff of Castle Head Field Studies Centre near Grange over Sands and, in particular, the owners: Mr and Mrs Dawson whose hospitality was so much appreciated during my hours of research.

I would also like to thank the English advisor from Bury, Jenni Saunders, who made the whole project possible.

Linda Hoy, 1989

For Colin

> *Three will fall claim to death's dark veil,*
> *Through greed of their own these men will fail*
>
> *One to Neptune's call will go;*
> *Nor for the second will he wait;*
> *the third the sands will hold below;*
> *The Attar Delve will seal their fate.*
>
> Lee Buckley
> Richard Smith

Each footstep was heavier than the last. He kept wanting to hesitate, to stop, to turn round, go back. The hardest thing was to keep clambering forwards into the sinking sands.

"Do you think we'll make it?"

No one answered. They were saving their energy, saving their breath, but as the tide came in and the sands squelched more and more, the reality was there. They had made a terrible mistake. They'd gone to the concert thinking they could return across the sands at night. They thought the way across would be easy. They'd scoffed at the suggestion that anyone might need a guide. And now the reality had dawned. The tide was rushing in much faster than they could walk. They weren't likely to reach the other side.

"Just keep going."

The mist was heavy as a sodden towel. The darkness

hung like a hungry bat as the moon hid behind a cloud. They'd lost sight of their landmarks, the specks of light on the coastal road. All they could do was stagger onwards as the sands sucked hungrily at their feet.

"Shouldn't we go back? Try another way..."

"No."

They couldn't go back because they knew what lay behind them: channels of biting water that had drained their strength as they swam across. Now the tide was rushing in, the channels would be impossible to cross.

"Keep moving."

All Kent Wilkinson had known before about quicksand was that, if you should ever get stuck, you mustn't stand still. You were all right so long as you kept moving. They'd joked about it earlier - before The Celtic Dead - because then it had seemed so easy. But what Kent hadn't realized was that to keep moving in the quicksands would be the hardest thing in the world. He wanted to stop, to have a rest, to test the sand with his feet, to look for a better way, to shout for help. Anything but lurch and slide, stickier and muddier with every step like a fly in a slurping well of treacle.

"I don't think we're going to make it." Warton's voice was desperate.

Kent tried to think of something reassuring but, in reality, he knew Warton was right. They were alone. Their teachers didn't know where they were; the three boys might not even have been missed yet. They'd made a terrible mistake. If only they'd stayed at Castle Head...if only they could have this evening back again...

Kent had never worried about dying. He didn't worry about it now. All he felt was sheer panic, a terror that liquified his body. If he didn't fall then possibly he might dissolve and slither, disintegrating inside the sand.

12

He imagined the wet grains swimming inside his nostrils and clogging up his throat.

"What's that?"

Arnold pointed ahead. There was a clearing in the mist.

Kent stopped. There was a shape. It was large and eerie. He felt faint with shock. Perhaps it was a ghost, an apparition of someone long drowned, someone who returned on misty nights intent on luring travellers to a watery grave. He tried to pull himself together. The shape was indistinct but it might just be a very large person, perhaps someone who'd come to their rescue. At the same time, there was a noise, a kind of humming and whirring, like a helicopter.

Kent stood still, straining his ears.

Perhaps someone had reported they were missing. Perhaps search parties had been out all evening. Perhaps this was their rescue helicopter and they were only seconds away from safety.

In his mind's eye, Kent could see the helicopter as it circled lower and lower. He could feel the warm blankets wrapped around him and the hot drink trickling down his throat.

He wanted to whoop with joy. "Here we are!" he began to shout.

But the words stuck in his throat. For as he tried to stagger forward, he found his feet embedded in the sand. He'd been standing still for too long and the sands were seeping round his ankles.

Sick panic rose into his throat. All this time he'd managed to keep moving. He'd only stood still for a couple of seconds and now it was as if he had taken root. He had to get free. He couldn't drown.

Kent summoned all his effort to pull and heave out his

right foot. But, as he did so, the sands gripped hold of his left. They covered his ankle and then the lower part of his leg. They were pulling him slowly and relentlessly like a hungry beast, reaching out its paws and dragging him into its slavering mouth.

"Aaagh!"

Kent toppled forwards on to the sands. He held out his hands to protect himself and then pushed downwards to keep his face from the water. He was overtaken by terror. He heard noises that sounded like the whining of a strange animal in pain and realized with shock that they were coming from him. Then the moon reappeared from behind the clouds. It reflected in the wet sands at his side.

And then Kent saw the paper. It must have been brought in by the tide. Floating on the water, was one of the thousands of leaflets printed to advertise the concert, the same leaflets he'd kept in his room to show his friends. Here it was, like the poster on his bedroom wall, and the logo on his T-shirt. Gazing up at him, out of the quicksand, loomed the three linked snarling serpents, the tail of one inside the mouth of another, eating and destroying, being destroyed and eating. The last thing Kent saw before losing consciousness was the famous ring of serpents: the family crest of the Wilkinsons and the sign of The Celtic Dead.

One

John looked at his pocket watch and saw that it was nearly time for tea. The fresh sea air always gave him an appetite. Hot muffins again, he hoped. He picked up his catch and his jumbo - the smooth wooden board on which he stood to rock the cockles to the surface. He was just about to leave the beach when he noticed a strange shape protruding from the sand. The welcoming thought of a plateful of hot buttered muffins almost made him turn away but, if there was one thing perhaps that marked John Wilkinson from any other young boy of 1740, it was his insatiable curiosity. He put down his jumbo and cockle basket and pulled the piece of metal from the sands.

It was very old, heavy and encrusted with barnacles, sand and rust. John walked a few steps to where there was a spring of fresh water, running into the bay. He dunked the piece of metal and rubbed it this way and that. He squinted at it in the failing light. There was little to see. Perhaps it was a buckle from someone's shoe or maybe part of the harness from a horse. What intrigued him was the notion that what he was looking at was an entwined ring of serpents, the tail of one in the mouth of another. He had seen similar designs before - Celtic patterns on embroidery and wallcoverings. His father might be pleased to see it. He put the metal clasp in the pocket of his breeches and set off home across the sands.

It was fifty years later when John Wilkinson met the

15

fortune-teller. He had taken his nephew to the fair. John was a sober, hard-working man with little time for frivolity, but today was a public holiday and he was in high spirits. "Come on then, Thomas," he cried as they stumbled from the ale-house into the brilliant afternoon sun, "we've put plenty of money away this week; let's see if we can't spend a little, eh?"

Thomas was surprised at the sudden change in his uncle's behaviour. It was a change that he remembered afterwards when he realized that this surely must have been the time when John had first learned of... mmm... and the fortun-teller... yes, of course. Everything fitted into place. But at the time, on that particular summer's afternoon, in his innocence, he suspected nothing at all.

Crowds had come from miles around. Thomas had seldom seen so many people all at once. The sudden explosion of sounds and smells and cries and squeals, mixed with his unaccustomed midday drinking, sent his brain round in a whirl. That was even before he saw the acrobats, balancing and tumbling in a pyramid and before he set eyes on Cadman the famous rope-dancer, flying through the air above them like a spider on a thread.

"Hot roast apples, all hot."

He could smell the roast apples before he heard the shout.

"Gingerbread! Come and buy your gingerbread!"

"Oysters! Fresh oysters!"

Both John and Thomas tried the coconut shy but the strange sounds and the dizzy atmosphere put both of them off the mark.

"Hot roast apples, all hot."

They bought a hot roasted apple each and then a plate of oysters. John kept laughing and slapping his nephew's back. "Come on, Thomas. Let's see the wax-works."

It was on their way to the waxworks that they passed the booth of the fortune-teller. "Hey! How about having your fortune told?" John asked him.

Thomas grinned and shook his head. His uncle was a scientist. What on earth had got into him today? He was the kind of man who would never dabble in such superstitious nonsense.

But after they had seen the waxworks, and the fattest man and the tallest woman in the world and paid to watch the man with the bagpipes and the dancing monkey in its little velvet jacket and matching breeches, they passed the fortune-teller's booth again. "Hey, come on," said John, "let's cross the gypsy's palm with silver." And for the twentieth time that afternoon, he took out his purse from the pocket of his waistcoat.

The booth was decorated on the outside with interlaced curling circles. Thomas found himself almost hypnotized as his eyes tried to trace the curving threads around the walls and up to the ceiling of the booth. It was hard to decipher the lettering across the doorway:

Rhiannon - teller of fortunes

From inside the booth, there came a gentle sound of humming:

Hm. Hmmmmmm. Hm. Hmmmmmmm.

Just then, Thomas's attention was distracted by a crowd of players. "The play's just starting!" he exclaimed. "Can we watch? I'd rather do that - if you don't mind."

17

John Wilkinson nodded. "I'll find you when I come out." He grinned. "If this woman really can see into the future, then she can tell me where to find you in the crowd."

As Thomas disappeared into the crowd, John listened again to the sound of humming:

Hm. Hmmmmmm. Hm. Hmmmmmmm.

It sounded like an old, familiar tune:

Hm. Hmmmmmm. Hm. Hmmmmmmm.
Alu La Lay
Hm. Hmmmmmm. Hm. Hmmmmmmm.
Alu Rhiannon

Inside, the booth was dark, lit only by a small green lamp. There was yellow smoke curling upwards and the strangest of smells - something like the incense of the High Church and something like the smell on the Liverpool quayside as ships unloaded their spices from the East. There was also an air of awesome calm. John almost trembled. Here, in the midst of all the noise and flurry of the fairground, it was as if he had suddenly found himself creeping into the silence of a tomb.

Rhiannon sat at a small wooden table on which stood an object covered by a velvet cloth. She lifted the cloth slightly and gazed inside. John expected the gypsy to tell him that he had an interesting face or that she would tell his fortune for an outlandish sum of money. But she said nothing. He wondered what she was staring at.

John gazed around the room. As his eyes became more accustomed to the dark, he noticed shelves stacked high with jars, some stone, some glass. Some seemed to contain dried herbs; others contained objects of such unusual shapes that...his gaze was transfixed by a jar which... perhaps it contained the rounded seeds of some strange plant, or...

"Sit down." Rhiannon motioned him to sit on a wooden chair.

John sat down, beginning to wish now that he had stayed outside with his nephew and the oysters and hot apples and the travelling players. All that seemed a world away from the confines and the silence of this booth.

"Can you give me something?"

John reached for his purse, beginning already to apologize that he had shown no sign of offering money.

The woman shook her head. "Something of yours," she said. "Let me touch something that is important to you. Something that you treasure."

John rummaged through his pockets. One contained his business cards - they were no good. Give the game away. He wanted her to guess, not read, about him.

The only object of any importance was his pocket watch. Solid gold and specially made to his design. He unfastened it and passed it across the table.

Rhiannon appeared not to look at the watch nor his hands nor the expression on his face, but her glance was crafty and well-rehearsed. As she sat in the shadows, half-hidden by her coloured shawl, she appeared to be gazing underneath the velvet cover at her crystal ball. But years of practice had taught her how to study a man. One brief glance could tell her the cost of the cut of his waistcoat, a glimpse of his face could tell her the number of hours he worked outside, and the touch of his hand as he handed over a watch could tell her how he earned his living.

The old woman nodded as she turned the watch over between her palms. She didn't appear to look at the watch; in fact it seemed to John as though something beyond his understanding - some memory, perhaps, some sense of movement was being transmitted into her mind.

Rhiannon was weighing the gold. "You are a hard-working man," she told him. "You have always worked hard."

John was impressed. He had expected her to assume that he had inherited his money and lived a life of leisure.

"You work with precision. You work with your hands."

This was quite amazing. No one could be more perceptive.

"And your work has brought you much success..."

John nodded. He gazed at her more keenly now, willing her to tell him more. For the first time, he could see her face clearly in the darkness. She seemed older than he first thought. Her face was lined and weathered, her eyes were deep-set and watering. She was wearing rings of silver in her ears and, around her shoulders, was a woven shawl of purple, gold and scarlet, patterned in a maze of circles like the Celtic design on the outside of her booth. Almost hidden beneath her shawl, he could just make out her long, grey, straggly, matted hair.

Suddenly, the woman looked directly at him. "There is a reason for your coming here today," she told him. "I believe that there is a question you wish to ask me."

John was not aware, of course, of being there for any reason, but then, when she said that, suddenly it was as clear as daylight. He nodded. It was as this point that the gypsy woman stretched out her hand for money.

John gazed round the room as Rhiannon stared into her crystal ball. His glance kept coming back to the jar with the strange seeds or...there was no getting away from it: they really did look like eyeballs. Perhaps the eyes of some large insect or reptile. Eyes of newt and Toes of Frog... he seemed to remember. Or was it, Claws of Newt and Eyes of Frog?

"You have been very successful," she told him. "Successful in business...isn't that true?"

"I'm an ironmaster."

"That's right, yes. I thought so. I said that you worked with your hands."

Rhiannon was gazing into the crystal ball, but still she kept turning over the watch. Suddenly, she held the watch where she could see it clearly, in the light of the lamp. The face was inlaid with jewels and a delicate painting of an iron bridge, but it was at the back that the woman stared. "What is this?"

"Oh." John shrugged. He was impatient now to hear about his fortune. "It's my emblem - a crest. I have it everywhere - on the boiler plates of my engines, on my writing paper, on my seal..."

"A ring of serpents..."

"It was a Celtic clasp. I found it when I was a young lad."

"Mmm." Rhiannon frowned. "Did you find it in the bay?"

"That's right."

"Mmmm." She hesitated. "This is an evil sign," she told him. "The sign of the Celtic Dead. It will bring bad luck."

John smiled and shook his head. "It seems to have brought me nothing but good luck so far."

"There's still time." She stared in silence at the watch.

21

"This watch tells me..."

John leaned forward.

"...I can see an iron coffin, a coffin being lowered into the ground." She looked up at John. "It doesn't seem to be in a churchyard. Do you know where it might be?"

John nodded. "My house at Castle Head. That's where I intend to be buried. The plans have been made. I shall be buried in an iron coffin."

Rhiannon shook her head. She spoke slowly and deliberately. "You will be buried three times," she told him.

John smiled and shook his head. This was a bit far-fetched. "I don't see why..."

"Three times," she insisted.

John began to fidget.

"You may be a successful man but money does not always bring happiness. You have few friends you can trust. And I see a woman, a young woman who is..."

John gasped.

"Isn't this where your question lies? Is this what you want to ask me?"

John found himself visibly shaking. How could she know? She had never met him before today. There was no one else in the world who knew about Anne and who knew about his hopes and disappointments.

"What is the question you have come to ask me?"

John hesitated.

The woman was staring hard at him. As she leaned slightly forward, he noticed something unusual about her posture. It was as if she had one shoulder slightly lower than the other.

John nodded grimly. "I have a large fortune but no heir. My wife is unable to bear a child. I was planning to leave my business and my fortune to my nephew but now, I am wondering... now that I have met, well..."

She waited.

"You see, I've met another woman who..."

"What is the question?"

John swallowed hard. "I want to know if there is any chance that I will one day father a son..."

Two

I change trains at Preston and stagger inside the buffet with my suitcase. *Travellers Fayre*, it says outside. It doesn't look very fair to me - everything is so expensive. I stand in the queue and gaze up at the notice:

Piping Hot Snacks
Freshly Cooked for You.

They must think we're stupid. "Freshly Cooked" means that this dozy-looking lad with ears like Prince Charles who looks as though he's been dragged by the lobes on to some government training scheme, puts the food in a cardboard carton and sticks it in the microwave. It ought to say, "Stale Food Warmed Up." Anyway, he can't even do that right. The man in front of me orders vegetable soup which Dumbo leaves on for nearly five minutes. All of us stand in the queue, staring at the soup through the little square window as it simmers and bubbles and then erupts like a miniature volcano, flooding the floor of the microwave. Big Ears looks quite amazed when he takes the carton out and finds it's completely empty.

I order a brunch muffin because it looks so wonderful and appetizing in the picture - sausage and cheese and tomato all piled up. I take it to a table on my own and sit down. What the pictures don't show is what the muffin looks like after your first bite. The melted cheese starts dribbling down my chin and the slices of tomato squirt out and land halfway down my shirt.

I sigh and try to wipe away the tomato stains. I'm starting my first job today and I was hoping to make a good impression.

When I've finished my muffin and coffee, I stagger back on to the platform for the train. The train I came on to Preston seemed quite normal; this one looks more like a toy. It only has two carriages with a seat for the driver at each end. I climb on at the back. The seats are nice and comfy but they're very old and torn and everything is dirty. The windows look like port holes in a dredger. I put my suitcase down then take out a tissue and try to wipe a space on the window clean enough to look out. I want to see where we're going.

We set off and sort of chug along, the way I expect those old-fashioned steam trains to go, but this one doesn't work on steam. Perhaps it might be clockwork. I notice that the driver's compartment in front of me is empty. I imagine the driver, squatting somewhere above me on the carriage roof feverishly turning round the key.

I gaze out of the clean space in the window. I want to be able to see the sea and the Blackpool Tower.

I can't see the sea but I do see some baby lambs. They don't have any lambs where I live. These are really tiny as if they've only just been born. They look like little wobbly pipe-cleaners. I wonder if there might be any lambs at Castle Head - that's the field studies centre where I'm going to work. It's in the country, on the edge of Morecambe Bay. I feel very excited about starting my first job and moving away from home. I hope it's going to be all right.

I keep looking at the label on my suitcase. My mother has insisted on printing my name on everything I own: Jenny Brown. Actually, my proper name is Jenny Lewis Brown but most people don't know about the Lewis. It was the name of my proper mother. I'm adopted, you see. One of the reasons why I wanted a job near the Lake District is because I've been wanting to find out where my real mother is. I know she comes from somewhere round there.

I feel embarrassed about having my name printed on all my belongings. It's as if I might not remember who I am. I think about when we were in the Infants and we always had to wear a name badge when we went out of school on a trip. It was in case we got lost and couldn't remember who we were.

Now I'm really on my own for the first time in my life and I know I have to look after myself. Nobody counts the people getting off the train to make sure we're all there. There won't be any teacher waiting on the station with a first aid box and sick bags and everybody's phone number. It isn't that nobody cares about me; it's just that I have to start to care more about myself.

The train stops at places I've never heard of: Arnside, Carnforth and Silverdale. We go through proper countryside with lots of fields and hills. I never do see the Blackpool Tower but, at last, I see the sea - the whole of Morecambe Bay, in fact, stretching out beside me. The bay is huge with lovely sands, smooth as chocolate. I always get excited about the seaside. It makes me think about going on holiday. When I was little, I always knew we were nearly there whenever I saw the sea.

Then something weird happens. I glance out of the other window - the side where I'm not sitting - and I see the sea. This is really confusing because that's the part where I thought it was land. Then when I look back through my window, there's sea below this side as well. It's just as if the train is skimming across the water. Of course I realize that there has to be a bridge. It's just that I can't see one. I can see lots of seagulls though, and ducks and sea birds with red legs, standing on islands of grass. Perhaps I'll learn the names of them later on. I can see the wide expanse of sand, as flat as an enormous slab of slate and I think how nice it would be to squelch across Morecambe Bay in my bare feet, leaving a trail of footprints like the ones you make in fresh white snow.

The train slows down and I see the sign that says Grange over Sands. We've arrived. I pick up my case and bags and step on to a platform that's so tiny and quiet, it reminds me of a station in a model railway layout. It has all the right buildings and people but there's so little noise that none of them seem alive. It's as if they're suspended in time. The change between Grange and the busy town where I live makes me feel lost and eerie. I hope I soon get used to it.

The first thing I do is to go over to look at the beach. The station is almost on the promenade, so I walk straight to the railings and look down. The tide is out, except for the stretch in the middle of the bay where we went across the sea on the train. I can see now where the bridge goes across the water with the railway lines on top of it.

The sands below me are covered in wavy lines, just as if someone's run across them with a giant comb. In the distance are large pools of water left by the tide, each of them as still as glass. It's late afternoon now and the sun's starting to go down and the pools reflect the colours of the sky: pink and purple, blue and orange. They remind me of mother-of-pearl: shells that are silky smooth inside, reflecting all the colours of the sunset.

At the side of me is a notice:

27

DANGER
BEWARE
fast-moving tides
quicksands
hidden channels.
In emergency phone 999 and ask for coastguard.

I think they must be exaggerating. The sands look perfectly safe to me.

I walk underneath the bridge to the taxi rank but, of course, there aren't any taxis. I bet a place like this only has one taxi anyway. It might not even have that. I decide I might as well walk. I came once before for my interview so I know the way already.

Last time, I got a lift to Castle Head from the station and it didn't seem very far, but of course I didn't have my suitcase then. Or my Sainsbury's carriers full of books. Or all the neatly-name-tagged woolly jumpers and thermal vests my mother's made me bring. She's got me kitted out like an Antarctic expedition. She's even stuck my hot water bottle in my case, the one with the furry snowman cover. If anyone sees it, I'll go spare.

I hobble round the corner past a posh hotel and straightaway it starts to rain - great big drenching drops. Oh no. Whilst I've been gazing dreamily over the sea, I've never noticed the dark clouds creeping over from inland. Perhaps it'll stop soon.

A car comes past and I think about thumbing a lift. My mum would go mad if she saw me hitch-hiking, but I don't want to turn up on my first day at work looking like a saturated wombat. Anyway, by the time I've heaved up my thumb with its two Sainsbury's carriers of assorted thermal underwear and snowmen hanging from it, the car's zoomed past.

I walk a bit further and stand in a place where I'm more visible, then I put my case and bags down and pose with my thumb in the air. I feel a bit stupid actually, but I'm starting to get drenched. A large van comes along and totally ignores me. It belongs to Cumbrian TV. I can't imagine what they're doing here; they're probably lost. Their programmes are always rubbish anyway. They probably zoom around with their eyes closed all day long.

The next thing is a minibus. And this one stops. Of course I have to go chasing after it up the road, which isn't easy with all my Antarctic expedition equipment but I feel really relieved when the driver opens the door for me.

"I'm only going as far as Castle Head," he tells me.

"That's where I want to be."

"Come on then, up you get."

I sit next to the driver ("Arthur" it says on his photograph over the mirror) and breathe out a sigh of relief. "Thanks a lot," I tell him.

He nods. "Are you going on one of these 'ere courses then?"

"No." I feel quite grown up telling somebody that I'm working. "I've got a job there," I explain.

He raises his eyebrows. "Well, rather you than me."

"How do you mean?"

"Well," he motions towards the back of the bus, "they'd never get me to spend three days looking after this lot."

I turn around for the first time and look at the passengers. All of them are boys, about sixteen or seventeen and they're covered in a haze of smoke. The back of the bus is ankle-deep in cans and empty crisp bags.

"Good gracious me, Arthur," one of them says in a really posh voice when he sees me. "We've picked up a half-drowned water rat."

"I think you should jolly well put her back again, Arthur," a very tall boy shouts at the driver. "You don't know where she's been."

"He's probably fished her up out of the sewer."

"If she's a pedestrian, I'd hate to see what the swimmers look like round here."

They all laugh at this as though they're being really funny. I think they're just ignorant.

Some of the boys are playing cards for money; some of them are singing songs that are much too disgusting for me to mention. When we steer past a rather wobbly lady on a bicycle, they shout and jeer at her and make rude signs through the window.

"Where've they come from?" I ask Arthur.

"Belmount Boys Boarding School."

I've never heard of it.

"Costs more money to send a lad there for a term than I earn in a year," Arthur grumbles. "And just listen to 'em." He shakes his head in disgust.

"Anyway," Arthur turns off the road into the long drive that leads to Castle Head. "I always believe that it's who you are that counts. It doesn't really matter where you come from."

I suppose he must be right.

"I hope you're not taking that rodent to Castle Head, Arthur," somebody shouts. "We'll be getting visits from the Environmental Health Department."

"How long are they here for?" I ask Arthur.

"Just till Sunday night." He pulls up outside the house. "But I think you'll probably find that's long enough."

I think he might be right.

Three

"Good morning, Humphrey Head here."

Humphrey sits on the edge of his bed, blow-drying his blond hairpiece. He is completely naked except for his black, silk smoking jacket.

"That's right, yes. Cumbrian TV."

He pours himself a glass of brandy.

"I'd like to talk to er...erm...Cecil, erm...what's his name..."

He struggles very hard to understand the regional accent of the woman on the telephone. He finds it very annoying that everyone doesn't speak in exactly the same way as him.

"The chappie who knows about the...er...what's its name...you know, dear, the sands and erm... He's not there?" Humphrey sighs rather loudly at the phone. "Fishing? What's he going fishing for? Hasn't he...doesn't he have any work to do?" He scowls at the telephone. "Oh, I see, it's his job, is it? Right, well, we'll have to catch him later on, then. Can we leave him a message? That's right, yes. Tell him Humphrey called, will you? Humphrey Head. Cumbrian TV."

He takes a long drink of his brandy.

"Thank you very much, dear. I'll give him a tinkle later."

The boys charge into the house. I can hardly believe that anyone can be so rude. They leave Arthur struggling to carry all their luggage and to clear the piles of rubbish out of the bus.

31

The rain is starting to ease off. I carry my bags into the hall, but when I see the surging mob of lads, pushing and shoving as they all try and find out where their rooms are, I decide to avoid being trampled in the crush and go back to give Arthur a hand.

"They ought to carry their own bags in," I tell him.

Arthur shakes his head. "No chance," he complains. "They're used to 'avin' a fleet of servants runnin' round after 'em, this lot are."

I smile. I hope he's exaggerating.

None of the boys have brought plastic carriers like mine. There are in-flight leather shoulder bags, designer sports bags and a couple of skiing bags. By the weight of them and the noise they make, I think most of them are filled with lager. Arthur staggers past me with some fishing gear and a couple of leather suitcases.

"I thought you said they were only here for the weekend?"

"That's right. If they were away for more than that, they'd have chartered a train."

I place a leather shoulder bag and a canvas hold-all in the tiled hallway next to an antique leather suitcase. I'm just about to turn back and fetch some more luggage when something strange catches my eye. Something unusual. In the top corner of the suitcase is a kind of crest - a sort of logo with a ring of serpents twisted round each other. It reminds me of something. I don't know what. I just think I've seen it somewhere before. I find myself staring at it.

"I don't suppose you'd care to carry them upstairs as well." It's the very tall boy who was speaking so rudely about me on the bus. He has this really posh voice that I've only ever heard comedians use when they're taking off the royal family and people like that. I assumed before that he was putting it on for a joke. I realize now with shock that he must speak like that all the time.

"I think you're big enough to carry them yourself," I tell him. I know that's rude but he's really put my back up. He should at least have said thank you to us for bringing them inside.

"Oh dear. Feeling a trifle miffed are we?" he says. He picks up the leather suitcase and carries it upstairs.

"Jenny! It's lovely to see you. Have you had a good journey?"

I nod and smile at Penny. "Yes thanks." Of course I've been half drowned and had to ride in a bus filled with the rudest boys I've ever met, but apart from that, the journey's been wonderful.

Penny puts her arm around my shoulder. "I'll make you a cup of tea," she says. Then she realizes how wet my clothes are. "Well, no, perhaps I'd better show you to your room first, then you can get changed. Can I take some of your bags?"

I feel embarrassed about my bulging Sainsbury's carriers when the rest of the hall is filled with antique leather suitcases and assorted designer luggage, but I'm pleased that Penny's being so nice. I felt a bit scared when I first came through the door.

We walk up the old-fashioned staircase. "Your room's on the corner," Penny explains. "That means you've got a view out on two sides."

I nod and try to think of something polite to say. "Thank you," is all I can manage.

"Here we are then." Penny opens the door to my bedroom.

Straightaway, my face drops because the room looks as though it's been furnished from a junk shop. The

33

furniture is the sort my grandma threw out years ago because she said it was too old-fashioned. I feel a bit disappointed but I try not to let it show.

"I should have a hot shower and get changed."

I nod at her and take my carriers. "Thank you very much."

"Look, Jenny...I did, erm...I did intend to give you the rest of today off but, actually we're very short staffed and there's this school party just arrived. I wonder if you'd mind giving us a hand with supper?"

"No, not at all."

"I don't want to rush you but, I mean, have a hot shower and whatever and come down when you're ready."

"Okay, I won't be long."

"I'll make you a cup of tea."

"Thanks very much."

I walk downstairs into the kitchen, put on an apron and wait for some instructions. "We're having curry and ratatouille today. Would you mind doing the mushrooms, Jenny?" Penny asks me, "And then chop up the onions and the garlic? You'll find them all in the fridge."

"Okay." I don't even know what ratatouille is but I search through the drawers for some vegetable knives and get started.

You might have thought, as I don't have many qualifications, that I'm just employed at Castle Head to work downstairs in the kitchens, but that isn't true. My job is a General Assistant. I'm only here on a trial period at the moment, but if they're happy with me, then I can have a permanent job.

Bernard, the owner, explained at my interview that I'd

do some domestic work - cleaning and cooking and making the fires - I'd help on the farm (I can't wait for that) and I'd work with the school parties as well, taking them rambling and canoeing. I just hope they don't ask me to do anything with Belmont Boys Boarding School brigade. I'd rather spend all week scrubbing out a sewer.

I wash the mushrooms properly but I don't bother peeling them; I hope that's all right. I'm not too sure what to do with garlic because my mum never uses it at home. My mum's a bit more traditional. She's very good at cooking Lancashire hot pot and steak and kidney pie but she doesn't go in for anything fancy. I peel the garlic and then it kind of falls apart into little chunks. I just chop them up a bit; I hope that's okay.

I find the onions in a brown paper bag. They look a bit small - not much larger than the onions my mum buys sometimes to pickle in jars; perhaps they've got more flavour than the big ones. I peel them and chop them up and put them with the garlic.

"Everything all right?" Penny reappears.

"Yes thanks."

"Well, if you've finished," she says, "Alli can do the ratatouille."

I smile at Alli. She's a rather tall lady with rosy cheeks.

"If you come with me, Jenny, I'll show you how to put the cheese and biscuits out upstairs."

I follow Penny up the staircase from the kitchen into the older part of the house. She shows me a big table outside the library. "Now," she explains, "we serve coffee and cheese and biscuits here for the adults when they come out of the upstairs dining room. You can arrange the cheese on the cheese board here and put out some plates of biscuits and then, when everyone's finished supper, fill some jugs with coffee and bring them upstairs. You can send them up in the dumb waiter if you like, and then collect them at the top."

I nod. I hope I manage to do everything all right.

When we go back to the kitchen, the ratatouille and curry are already in the oven and I have to put out all the crockery and knives and forks. I can already hear the boys crowding outside the door.

"Hey, Warton, is it true that your old man drives a Lada?"

Warton's protests are hidden beneath the blaring of heavy metal on someone's ghetto blaster.

"I say, I say, how does one double the value of a Lada?"

"I don't know, old chap. How does one double the value of a Lada?"

"Fill it up with petrol! Ha, ha, ha!"

I hear the boys crack up laughing as though it's the funniest thing they've heard all week.

"Why are we waiting? Why...y...are we waiting...Why are we wai...ai...ting oh, why, why, why...?

I try not to feel annoyed. It's only ten to six and supper isn't supposed to start until six o' clock.

"I say, I say, what does one call a Lada with a sunshine roof?"

"I don't know. What does one call a Lada with a sunshine roof."

"A skip."

"Ha, ha, ha."

"Would you like to eat upstairs with us, Jenny? It'll be a bit less noisy then."

I take off my apron then follow Penny into the upstairs dining room and straightaway, I feel like running straight back out again. The room is vast, with an

36

enormous table in the middle and about fifteen people sitting round.

"Oh, hello, Jenny." Bernard stands up when I walk in and finds me a seat. He's the man in charge of Castle Head who asked all the questions when I came for my interview.

This is Jenny," Bernard introduces me to everyone.

"You know Penny?"

I nod.

"And Alli..."

I smile at her.

"Would you like to sit down?"

"Thank you."

Alli moves up to make room for me.

"And these are some of the teachers from Belmount Boys School."

I smile and look sympathetic.

I sit gazing round me open-mouthed. It's like I imagine the rooms to be in Buckingham Palace. And there are so many nice things to eat on the table that I don't know where to start.

"Would you like some curry?" Bernard passes me a big tureen and I start to help myself. I hope I don't drop it or do anything stupid.

"Will you have some rice?" asks Alli.

"Thank you."

There's a large blue tablecloth and then another white lacy cloth in the middle. Right in the centre are blue candles in silver candlesticks.

"Some chutney?"

"Thank you."

At one end of the room is an enormous marble fire-place with a log fire burning. Well, when I say "logs", they look bigger than most of the trees in our local park.

"Would you like some banana slices?"

"Thank you." I've never had bananas with curry before but I don't want to show myself up.

"Can I pass you some salad?"

"Thank you."

"Did you have a good journey here?" asks Alli.

"Yes, thank you." I feel embarrassed that I can't think of anything to talk about. I know I ought to make conversation but I can't think what to say.

"Coconut?"

"Thank you." I've never had coconut with curry either but there's always a first time. I sprinkle some over my bananas.

"What about all the boys that came in the bus?" I ask Alli at last. "Do they always eat downstairs?" I'd feel happiest if she told me that they've all just been sent home for bad behaviour.

"That's right," she explains. "This dining room is just for adult visitors and staff."

Well, that's a relief, anyway.

"Would you like some ratatouille?"

I've never been offered two main courses before. "I'll perhaps have some after my curry," I tell her. I haven't really got room on my plate for anything else.

I'm still sitting awe-struck, gazing round the room, but I try to keep my mouth closed as I'm eating.

In front of me are three long, tall windows which open out on to the verandah. The pelmets are carved and painted in gold. But the most amazing thing about the room is the ceiling which is painted all over with cherubs and fruit. In the centre is an eight-pointed star with the white plaster heads of men and women from long ago.

"You haven't had any potatoes, Jenny, have you?"

38

"I don't think I've got room for any thank you."

There are bunches of painted fruit stuck on the ceiling. Again, I think they must be made of plaster.

"Would you like some ratatouille now?"

"Well, I'll just have a little bit, thank you."

After the first course, we take our dirty plates over to a table in the corner and pull up the pudding through a hatch. There are two little doors in the wall and, when you open them, there's a small lift inside. Alli pulls on one of the ropes and trays appear with pudding bowls on. "Have you ever worked one of these before?" she asks me.

"I've never seen one before."

"It's called a dumb waiter. They're a good idea. A lot of big old houses used to have them."

For dessert, we have a choice between trifle, chocolate gateau, peaches, and profiteroles. Nobody seems to mind if you have all four. After I've lived here for a month, I'll probably burst.

Four

"Well, the chocolate gateau was very nice," Penny compliments Alli, as she bustles into the kitchen with a pile of clean tea towels.

"Thanks."

"The curry had a strange taste to it, though. I wasn't sure what it was..."

"Mmmm." Alli looks puzzled. "I felt as though there was something not quite right, somehow."

I'm busy sorting out the knives and forks. There's a bowl of soapy water left on the hatch for the boys to put their cutlery in. They've managed to put cutlery in it, but also bits of chocolate gateau, peas and bits of carrot and curry. I can't believe how stupid they are. I take the separated cutlery over to the sink.

"Hey! Who's supposed to be helping wash up?" Penny shouts through the hatch into the dining room.

The only boys left are Warton and his rather podgy friend who are stuffing themselves with extra helpings of chocolate gateau and cream. The others have scarpered off.

"I'll go and fetch Kent," Warton offers.

"No, you won't," Penny tells him. "You two can help on your own. The others can do it tomorrow."

"They'll be about as useful as a pair of chocolate teapots," Alli mutters.

"Never mind," says Penny. "They've still got to do their share. And if we let them go out through the door, I don't think we'll see them again."

The fat boy ambles into the kitchen. "What's your

40

name?" Alli asks.

"Arnold. Arnold Thwaite."

"Right, Arnold, here's your tea towel."

I start to make the coffee to take upstairs and Penny opens the fridge to take out the cheese. Then she stands and frowns. She takes a large string bag of onions out of the bottom of the fridge. "You didn't use these, Jenny?" she asks me.

My stomach sinks. I've got a horrible feeling that I might have done something wrong. I shake my head. "I used the other ones," I explain.

I can see Penny and Alli exchanging glances and I start feeling worried. "Where did you find them?" Penny asks me.

I can't see why it's so important whereabouts I found the onions but I explain. "They were in a brown paper bag," I tell her. "On the shelf by the draining board."

Penny's mouth drops open in shock. I know I've done something awful. "On the shelf up there?" she points.

I nod. I can feel myself going bright red.

Alli looks worried as well. "What's the matter, Penny?" she asks.

"You know the tulip bulbs we bought before Christmas?"

"The ones we never got round to planting..."

"Yes, I decided to save them for next autumn..."

I can see the look of horror creep across Alli's face.

"Jenny's cut up all the tulip bulbs," Penny explains. "She's cut up the tulips and we've all eaten them in the curry."

I wheel my trolley along the tiled corridor towards the library, wishing I could dissolve. I know my face is like a bowl of tomato soup.

"Ah, coffee's on it's way everyone, Marjorie!"

I park the trolley and try to start pouring out the coffee, but the cup and saucer shake together like a pair of dentures in a blizzard. I don't think I'll ever live this down.

"I'll just get another saucer."

There's more coffee landed on the saucer and in the biscuits than in this chap's cup. I can't find a serviette so I discreetly place my sleeve over the biscuits in the hope it'll soak up some of the coffee I've spilled. "There's some cheese there if you'd like some."

I thought Penny might sack me but she hasn't; she just made a big joke about it and told Bernard when he came downstairs and everybody laughed. I knew I had to join in the fun as well but I was really only pretending. I just felt mortified. All I wanted to do was run upstairs and hide.

"There's cream over there as well." As I point out the cream jug, I notice two digestive biscuits sticking to the underside of my sleeve. "Would you like some Gorgonzola?"

I scrape the biscuits off my sleeve and slide them in my pocket, then I concentrate hard on aiming coffee into cups. I find it's best to do this if I stand the cups on the trolley; they don't shake about as much then.

"When it's Spring again I'll sing again..."

I think I know what's coming. Out of the corner of my eye I see Kent and Arnold walking down the stairs towards the library.

"...tulips from Amsterdam."

I start to decompose.

"When we meet again, we'll eat again..."

I put down the coffee jug with as much dignity as I can muster.

"...tulips from Amsterdam!"

Then I turn around and walk as serenely as I can up the Regency staircase in the direction of my bedroom. I don't even look at Kent and Arnold.

"When we're here again, we'll fear again..."

I walk down the corridor to my door.

"...tulips from Amsterdam!"

Then I run inside my room, close the door and throw myself down on the bed. I squash my hands around the pillow and hide my head underneath the covers.

The first night on my own is strange. I've never slept away from home by myself before. I've only been on holiday with my mum and dad.

When I first saw my room, I felt disappointed because the furniture was so old. My bed is made of dark wood with an iron frame like the one my grandmother used to have before she moved into her new flat. The wardrobe is like a big dark wooden box; it reminds me of a coffin standing on its side.

But then, you see, Castle Head is very old. It has high ceilings and dark woodwork everywhere. A lot of the floors are made of polished, painted tiles. I don't suppose it would look right if they filled it with modern furniture. When I open the curtains to look outside, everything is dark, completely black. I'm not used to that. I'm used to street lights and the sound of traffic.

I fill up my snowman hot water bottle, snuggle up in bed and try to forget that everything's so strange. I'd expected the house to be quiet - which it is - it's really peaceful, except for the din that all the horrible boys are making. I hear their shouts, first of all, in the distance as they walk back from the village - from the pub, no doubt. Then there are footsteps pounding down the corridors and the sound of banging doors echoing round the house and making the windows rattle. Just when I think I can relax and get some sleep, taps are turned on, toilets start flushing, people start making cups of tea and somebody switches on their tape recorder.

In another sense, I'm pleased to have some noise around me. Like I say, I've never slept on my own before, away from my mum and dad, and the house is very strange. It's hard to get used to the high ceiling and the dark heavy shapes of the furniture. As I'm hoping to stay here for a long time, I'd like to make the room more personal. When I go home for the weekend, I'll take down some of the posters from my bedroom wall and bring those. I don't think anyone here will mind. I'll perhaps bring some of my plants as well. And my mobiles. I start to think about how it will look with all my own things here. I'd like to bring Gary Glitter, my goldfish, but I don't know how I could carry him on the train.

I start to fall into a dream. I'm running after a clockwork train and I'm carrying two suitcases, a pile of posters, a mobile, two spider plants and balancing Gary Glitter and an enormous cheese plant on my head.

I'm almost asleep when I hear the voice. I don't think it's anything unusual at first because there are so many noises all round. I can hear an owl hooting outside my window and footsteps running down the corridor and so I don't think it's strange when I hear the voice of a young woman passing just outside my door:

He said how it would bring me luck, but I'm not sure now. I don't know, not after what Mary told me. He said, "Take this 'ere ring of serpents with thee, and this can be a sign for ye. This can be your good luck charm, my sweetheart." But I know not what to think of it now.

The first picture in my mind is of the crest I saw earlier on the tall boy's suitcase. That's what I think of when I hear her talk about the ring of serpents. Then I see a picture of her. It doesn't occur to me to wonder how I know what this person looks like when I've never even seen her before, but the picture I have is of someone from long ago. Everything about her is old-fashioned. She's very young but the way she talks sounds more like my grandma and her friends from the Golden Age holiday club.

When Mary saw where I had it hidden in amongst all the bits of worsted for the little one she turned round on me all come over strange. "What be this then?" she say. And when I tell her how it be a good luck charm she shake her head as if all in disbelief. "This no bring you luck, my dear," she tell me. "This here be an evil charm; it be the sign of death. This here be the evil sign of the Celtic Dead drowned inside the sands."

I think she must be a servant. She's wearing an apron that reaches to her feet over a long dark skirt. The apron has a little bib, but no straps. It must be pinned on to her top. She has a low neckline with a white neckerchief, almost as wide as a shawl, and on her head she wears a kind of bob cap with white lace round the edges. She's small and slim; I don't think she's much older than I am, but her face looks worn and worried.

So now I know not what to think. If I could write 'e a letter I could tell him. But I fear he would think me foolish. I will have to wait until I see him and I know not how long that will be.

I don't feel afraid of the woman; there doesn't seem anything spooky about her; it's just the fact that she's there and yet she's not there; I seem to know her and yet I don't; I seem to see her and yet, of course, I can't.

Maybe I've had too much to think about for one day. I fall asleep and dream about Gary Glitter.

Five

I look out of my bedroom window at a vast expanse of countryside. At home, all I ever saw from my room were the houses and the lampposts on the opposite side of the street. It's almost as though I've been living inside a box and now the roof has been lifted off and I can see the world outside. The world is big and green and has a vast expanse of sky and there are mountains on the horizon. I just can't get used to the countryside; I can't get used to the stillness and the quiet and the fact that nothing much seems to happen. When I look out of my window, for instance, the only things that move are some sheep and a few baby lambs and a big red bird like a hen. I think that it might be a pheasant. And the river, of course; that moves as well. The river flows in a perfectly straight line in front of my window as though someone has dug a channel for it. Behind it are flat fields and then the hills that I think are the bottom part of the Lake District.

I go downstairs to help make the breakfast. I have to fry hundreds of eggs on a hotplate that's the size of a small tennis court and grill stacks of sausages and bacon at the same time. With my other hand, I'm stirring an enormous pan of porridge on the cooker. "Make sure it doesn't burn on the bottom," Alli tells me.

It had better not. I can't bear the shame of doing anything else that's really stupid. If I make any more mistakes, I'll just go home.

I put out Corn Flakes and Coco Krispies on the tables and then fill the milk jugs, take out all the cereal bowls

47

and then I have to start making twenty pots of tea. I have to keep stirring the porridge as well.

I can hear the Belmount blockheads staggering down the stairs. I can hear Kent Sands anyway.

"Wonder what's for brekkies, hey chaps...a portion of grilled trout? Devilled kidneys? A few slivers of smoked salmon? Oh look, it's Coco Krispies and porridge. Well, never mind..."

Kent walks in. He's wearing a pair of black and yellow lycra overalls that only come down to his knees and are held up with silly braces. He has a yellow shirt underneath with a zip under his chin. When I look towards the bottom of his legs, he's wearing skiing tights under the overalls and what I think are rock climbing boots. He reminds me of an Austrian goatherd.

"Like the salopettes, Kent!" Someone shouts across.

"Trendy, aren't they?" Kent twiddles round and poses with his bowl of porridge. He looks like a refugee from The Sound of Music.

But when I see Arnold (that's Kent's fat friend), wearing knee length, skin-tight, pink and purple shorts and matching rock boots and a pair of dark glasses - all this, by the way, is just for sitting and eating his Coco Krispies - I have to run back inside the kitchen before I collapse with hysterics.

"Good Grief!" says Alli. "Have you seen them all? They must have brought thousands of pounds worth of expedition equipment. I'm sure they're only going for a walk!"

"I say, Warton, why does your father drive a Lada?" I hear Kent's voice through the hatch. "Is that all he can afford?"

Poor old Warton is still trying to deny that his father has even contemplated buying a Lada.

"I say, chaps, why do you have a heated rear wind-screen on a Lada?"

"I don't know, Kent. Why do you have a heated rear windscreen on a Lada?"

I start to dollop the fried eggs, sausage, bacon and fried bread out on the heated plates.

"To keep you're hands warm when you're pushing it!"

"Ha. Ha. ha." They all seem to find that hilarious.

Each plate has to have one egg, two sausages, three pieces of bacon and two squares of fried bread.

"Morning, Tulip!" Kent sticks his head inside the serving hatch.

I don't sav anything.

"Do you think we could order some devilled kidneys?"

I sigh. "It's eggs, sausage and bacon," I explain, handing him a plate.

"Don't we get any fried tulips today then?"

"Tulips are off today," I tell him.

"How about snowdrops? Snowdrops on toast?"

I just swallow hard.

"How about daffodils? Haven't you any little mignons of sautéd daffodils...perhaps in a kind of mushroom sauce with..."

Everyone else is queuing up. I push the plate into his hands. "Come on," I tell him impatiently. "There are other people waiting."

I don't relax until I see the Belmount boys brigade setting off on their walk, weighed down with ice picks, ropes and safety helmets. The equipment looks so heavy that, if they fell into the quicksands, I think they'd be sucked straight down to the bottom. Not that any-body'd be too upset, mind you.

*   *   *

I spend most of the morning unpacking the rest of my things. Then I walk around the the grounds of Castle Head. Alli has told me that two new baby lambs have been born in the night and I really want to see them. I feel very lucky to get a job here; it seems such a wonderful place to work. I've always wanted to work in the country and to do something with animals.

I run behind the farmyard, along a pathway that leads to the field where the sheep are. I can see the lambs straightaway. They look really tiny. I open the gate and stride across the muddy grass to inspect them. I really want to pick up the baby lambs and hug them but I think I'd better not. Two of the lambs are white and fluffy. They keep diving under their mother for a feed and then they run about, stumbling on the hummocks of grass. Then there are two tiny black lambs, weeny bundles of curly, black wool, that have only just been born; they're still sticky because their mum hasn't cleaned them properly yet. They're even wobblier when they stand up because they haven't even had time to learn how to use their legs.

The black lambs look a bit weaker than the others. I hope they'll be all right.

When I've been to see the lambs and had a bit of lunch, I still have a couple of hours free so I decide to do some more exploring.

Behind the house is a small steep hill, covered in trees, with a pathway leading straight up to the top. Most of it is like a wilderness with ivy and other creepers everywhere. I set off climbing, my wellies squelching in the mud.

All around me are very big trees. I don't know what sort they are, but I think they must be very old. The wood is dense. I can see lots of pathways but most of them are overgrown; only the big steep path that I'm walking on is clear.

I still find it hard to get used to the fact that everything's so quiet; but then, of course, in another sense, it isn't quiet at all. There are just different kinds of sounds, different noises from the ones you hear in towns - sounds like the wind in the trees and the song of birds.

Today, I can hear the low hum of traffic in the distance; I can hear the bleating of sheep and the chirping and singing of all the different birds. I'd like to buy a bird book so I can start getting to know some of their different names.

Suddenly, there's a crackling in the leaves right next to me. It makes me jump. I turn round startled, just in time to see a big fat rabbit, bounding away with its white tail bobbing

After a while, the path becomes very steep and it looks as if, at one time, there were steps - there are broken flat rocks to walk on and, in the wall beside me are metal rings which I think might once have supported a handrail or a rope. It doesn't matter that the handrail's gone. I can climb the steps without one. I think you would only need something to lean on when it's icy.

I pause to take a breath and have a look around. It's like a different world up here. There are more and more creepers everywhere; some of them have their roots wrapped around the trunks of giant trees; they look dry and old, like gnarled intestines.

And then I notice something strange. There's a big tree in front of me that has a carving on it, near the top. That's not unusual because I've seen bits of carving and initials on quite a few other trees. I think you get that

51

everywhere where they've had lots of children staying. But what catches my eye about this one is the design. It's the ring of serpents, the tail of one inside the mouth of the next. It's carved very carefully. Someone must have sat up on a high branch of the tree for a long time with a pocket knife, cutting it out of the bark. I can't think why they'd want to do that. It reminds me of the woman I heard last night. She talked about a ring of serpents. It also makes me feel strange because I feel sure now that I've seen the design before somewhere, apart from on Kent's leather case. I wonder if I might have seen it in a film, or seen it carved on a building somewhere; but the feeling I have is that the only place I've seen the design is in a dream. It's like a very distant memory. It's like when you wake up sometimes and you can remember the feeling of the dream you've just had, but not what it was about. And the more you try to remember, the further it goes away.

At the base of the tree, someone has carved the initials J.W.. I can't think who that could be. I take a few deep breaths and then start to climb higher up the hill. The path looks quite well used, but the woods on either side are impenetrable, like the woods around the Sleeping Beauty.

I stop and listen. My heart skips a beat. There's a strange noise in the undergrowth. When I stop, the noise seems to stop but when I start walking I hear it again. It's a kind of crackling, like the sound of someone's footsteps on the leaves. I listen and then I peer into the dark shadows of the woods, but I can't see anyone. I think it must be rabbits, scampering through the leaves.

The path leads around a crumbling high wall. The wall, or what is left of it, is curved, like the rounded turret of a castle. At one point, there's a seat, a wooden bench built into the wall like a kind of old-fashioned country bus shelter. But you'd have a long wait for a bus up here.

I sit on the bench and look around. I think that once, a long time ago, it would have been a lovely place to sit. The roof is patterned with pieces of rustic wood, like a sort of mosaic of squares and diamonds. There are a few pieces left on the wall behind me, but most of them have dropped off. Slices of the wood are lying on the ground, covered in woodworm. On most of the wall, only the rusty nails are left, drooping from the brick work like encrusted brown bogies. I look the other way instead.

I feel sure that, a long time ago, there would have been a beautiful view from here. I think that's why they must have built the seat. It's very high up and the surrounding countryside is flat, so I bet you'd have been able to see for miles. Now that everything has grown so wild, all I can see are trees.

Six

"Would you mind going in to serve behind the bar please, Jenny?" Penny asks me. "The teachers would like a drink before they give their talk."

I've never served behind a bar before so I've no idea what to do. "Yes, of course," I tell her. They'd better not want cocktails or anything complicated. I had enough problems serving the coffee and biscuits.

"Oh, right-i-ho there. Barmaid's here," says this obnoxious-looking chap in glasses and flared trousers. "What'll you have, Marjorie?"

"A pint of bitter, please, Doctor."

They both crack out laughing at this as though it's the funniest thing they've said all day.

Anyway, I know which are pint glasses because they're the big ones with a handle at the side. I place one underneath the tap marked Best Bitter and wait for it to fill up. For reasons I can't understand, when there's still only about two centimetres of beer at the bottom of the glass, the froth whizzes up the sides like a pan of boiling milk and begins to disgorge itself right down my legs, through my trainers and my socks. I place the beer mug swiftly on the counter. "There you are." I say smartly. I try to ignore the overflowing froth which quickly floods out the top of the bar and trickles down on to the deep pile carpet.

"Oh, er...thank you very much." Marjorie looks a bit uncertain. "Well, I'll look all right with this, eh what?" She lifts up the mug and chortles at the dizzy doctor. They both break out laughing again although I still can't see the joke myself.

"What are you having then, Dr Lune?"

Dr Lune! Perhaps they call him that because of his flared trousers.

"I'll have a Scotch please."

I'm about to say, "Scotch what?" but I try to use my brains instead. Behind me is a giant bottle of whisky hanging upside down. It has a picture of a Scottish glen complete with reindeer on the label. "Will this be all right?" I gesture in the direction of its antlers.

"Yes, fine thanks."

Getting down the bottle to pour it out looks complicated. It would probably involve a set of spanners, a screwdriver, a small crane and taking half the wall apart. Then I realize there's a kind of dispenser at the bottom. I've seen people do this on the telly.

I find a half pint glass, place it under the mouth of the bottle and press upwards. Some of the whisky spurts out but it hardly covers more than the bottom of the glass. I give it about six more squirts but there still doesn't look to be very much. "Would you like some water or anything with it?" I ask hopefully.

"No thanks, it'll be all right by itself."

I give it another three or four squirts and hand him the half-full glass. I hope he won't be disappointed.

"Er...thank you," he says, a bit uncertain. "How much ...er...how much is it?"

I check the price of a glass of whisky on the list and tell him.

"Oh, right, very generous," he says. He seems to be happy enough.

Then Penny puts her head round the door and beckons me. "Would you mind just sorting out the library, Jenny? Dr Lune's giving his talk in there in a few minutes."

I follow Penny out into the corridor.

"It's a bit untidy. Perhaps you could put the chairs round in a circle and leave some water out for him and... oh yes, he said he might need the blackboard. It's in the lecture room."

I've tidied the library once already before tea but, now the Belmount boys have been in there, it looks like the wake of a nuclear holocaust. I pick up their magazines, put their empty cans into the bin, stack some logs on the fire, draw the curtains then go to fetch the blackboard and easel.

I come back to find Kent and Warton lounging with their feet up on the tables and another semi-circle of empty Coke cans on the floor.

"Oh, I say. It's Winnie the Water Rat," Warton chortles, loud enough for people to hear in Morecambe. "Dried out now, have we?"

I thought the Water Rat was yesterday's joke. I don't say anything at all. I just try to ignore them.

"Lost our tongue, have we? Or have we left it behind us somewhere in the drainage system?"

I sigh very deeply and try to keep my temper. I struggle to stand up the easel and peg the blackboard in its place.

"I say, if that's one of the friendly, hospitable members of staff we read about, I'd hate to see what the un-friendly ones are like."

I just try to take no notice.

"What's happened to Loony Bin?" asks Kent. "He said he'd be here at half past."

Then Arnold rolls in with a bag of crisps in his hand, trailing them across the carpet as he makes his way to the settee.

I try to keep calm. I go and fetch a jug of water and a

glass and place them on the coffee table at the front.

The rest of the boys have arrived now and the noise is unbearable. There's a game of Pontoon going in the corner and a cacophony of heavy metal from Kent Wilkinson's ghetto blaster. I decide I'd better try and drag their teachers out of the bar. I can't tidy the library again with all these hooligans in it.

"Now, now lithen to this, Marshory. W...what do you call a ... call a Latha with a thun woof?"

"I don't know Doctor. What do you call a Latha with a thun woof?"

"No. No. I mean, what do you ..."

"The boys are waiting in the library," I tell him.

Dr Lune blinks at me as though I've just beamed down from outer space.

"We ought to be going through," Marjorie explains.

"No, no a...Lada...it's a..."

"Come on." She tries to tug him by the arm.

"No, no a Latha with a thun woof..." He bursts into huge guffaws of laughter when he suddenly thinks of the punch line to his joke. "It's a thip, gethit?"

"A ship? Oh, very funny."

"No, it's a..."

Marjorie gestures me to help her and we take an arm each and start to steer the doctor towards the library door.

We position the doctor behind the coffee table where he sways backwards and forwards looking rather seasick.

Marjorie blinks at the conglomeration of Pontoon playing, Viz viewing louts. "Come on, boys," she tells them curtly. "Sit up straight."

Some of them glance upwards and Kent turns down

the sound of Iron Maiden.

"Now," says the Doctor. "The place where we're thtaying is thouth of the Thake Disthrict." He swallows hard and then frowns uncertainly at the curtains. "Morecambe Bay - an area of thoo hundred thquare miles..."

"Can we have that in kilometres please, Doctor?" asks Arnold trying to look as though he's interested.

"Mmm. Wight-i-ho. An area of two hundwed thware kilometres..."

He sees Marjorie rapidly shaking her head in horror.

"No, no, just a minute..." The Doctor removes a calculator from his breast pocket and stares at it quizzically.

"The thwitch is at the thop, thir," Arnold reminds him.

Doctor Lune switches on his calculator. "Now who can thell us," he asks, "how many miles there are in a kilometre?"

There's silence for a moment then a small boy wearing a tie and sitting in the front row actually raises his hand.

"Yeth, Thandy?"

"A kilometre is five eighths of a mile, Doctor Lune, sir," he explains.

"Hmmm, right then..." Dr Lune presses the buttons on his calculator. "Thoo hundred thimes five is...one thousand and then, multhiplied by eight gives us...let's thee, that's eight thousand thquare kilometres."

Several people grin at this but no one actually corrects him.

Just then, Dr Lune notices the jug on the coffee table. He lifts the jug high in the air and stares at it. He does this for quite some time.

"If this is supposed to be one of the professional

58

academic members of our staff," chuckles Warton, "I'd hate to see what the raving idiots look like."

The Doctor now seems to have gone into a hypnotic trance. Marjorie looks worried.

Suddenly, Dr Lune notices the drinking glass. He lifts it up and, with a sudden flash of recognition, starts to pour water towards it from the jug. Unfortunately, it misses the glass completely. In an attempt to realign himself, Dr Lune topples forward, spilling most of the water over Sandy, sitting speechless in the front row.

"Oh, I'm therribly thorry."

He takes out a large dirty handkerchief and staggers forward in Sandy's direction, leaning on the blackboard for support. Then Sandy stands up to try and shake the water from his shirt. As he sees the doctor's dirty handkerchief-filled paw reaching out towards him, he takes a sudden step backwards and Dr Lune stumbles, catching his legs on the easel as he falls. I close my eyes as the easel crashes to the ground. When I dare to look again, all I can see is the blackboard lying on the floor with a pair of flared trousers sticking out from underneath.

I decide that perhaps I ought to send for Bernard.

Seven

"Right," says Bernard, "I'll tell you a bit about the history of Castle Head."

The boys are now sitting smartly in rows, facing the front of the room. Their magazines and playing cards have been put out of sight and Kent's tape recorder has been placed in solitary confinement between the legs of the coffee table under Bernard's watchful eye. Dr Lune has gone upstairs to lie down and Marjorie has taken him a bucket to be sick in - just in case.

Bernard's evil eye tracks round the room, as he makes sure that no one is going to misbehave. "Well," he starts off, "this house was built in 1781 by John Wilkinson. He was an ironmaster who worked with James Watt and Matthew Boulton on the production of steam engines, but the actual history of the estate goes back much further." He pauses and looks round once again to make sure that everyone is paying attention. "Behind the house, as you've all seen, is a small steep hill which - it's assumed - was the site of an ancient iron-age fort. There've been many Celtic remains found in the area and, in fact, there's a local legend about a whole Celtic army going down into the sands. I don't know if you want to hear about all that..."

Bernard hesitates, but everyone is nodding with enthusiasm, waiting to hear about the Celtic bodies in the sands.

"Well, there were two tribes living in the area: the Novantae in the north - these were the people who would have lived at the hill fort here - and then in the south were the Brigantae. The Celts were a warlike people and there were lots of skirmishes and battles between the different tribes. Anyway, according to the story, the Brigantae were trying to invade. They captured the guide - the chap whose job it is to show people across the sands - and they forced him to plant a trail so they could find their way across the quicksands at night and invade the hilltop fort.

"Now, in fact, this thing about the guide is interesting because we do, actually still today have a guide across the sands. His name's Cedric Robinson and he lives in a cottage - Guide's Farm it's called - just a mile or so up the coast."

Bernard raises his arm and points towards the bar across the corridor but, if we were outside, I suppose he'd be pointing in the direction of Grange over Sands.

"The sands here are very hazardous - I'll tell you more about that later - there are sudden deep channels, quicksands and the tide can come in very quickly - it's easy to imagine you can walk across the bay at low tide and then find yourself completely cut off. There's a local tradition that the earliest guide was employed during the reign of King John, but, in fact, the earliest record we have is from 1501. A chap called Edmonson was known as the "Carter upon Kent Sands" presumably because he used to take people across in a horse and cart. Most of the other guides since then have had the name of Carter and Guide's Farm is actually situated on Carter Lane.

"Now what Cedric does before he takes anyone across the sands is to go out on his own and plant sprigs of laurel - outside Guide's Farm is a hedge of laurel. He works out which is the safest way across - it'll change you see, according to the tides and the time of year and how much rain there's been - all kind of things - and

61

then he'll plant these laurel branches in the sand - brods is the local name for them - and these should withstand three or four tides..."

Sandy, still sitting on the front row with his wet shirt, raises his hand. "Could you spell that, Mr Wharfe, please sir?"

"Yes, of course. B..r..o..d..s."

Sandy, I notice, has his exercise book out and is taking notes. Some of the others look interested, but quite a few of them seem to be drifting off to sleep. I'm beginning to think the meals at Castle Head might be a bit too generous.

"Well, just to go back to the story, the legend is that the Brigantae captured the guide - of course, we don't even know whether they had a guide in those times or not, but anyway, that's how the story goes - and forced him to go out and mark the way across the sands so they could approach the hill fort at night."

Kent has fallen asleep. His head is lolling forward on his chest, like a marionette with a broken string. His mouth is wide open as well. I hope he doesn't start to snore

"This legend is actually one of the many surrounding the Celtic character, Rhiannon. She features in a lot of Celtic stories but she appears under different guises - in this story, we see her as a slightly deranged old woman dancing round the beach at night."

I try to gesture to Warton to give Kent a little nudge, but then I realize that Warton looks half asleep as well. They'll probably both be full of energy in half an hour ready to zoom off to the pub.

"When she sees the laurel branches, she picks them up like a little girl gathering flowers. She kind of waltzes round, stopping and picking up the brods, twirling round and planting them somewhere else. Of course, the Brigantae have no idea that anyone's moved the brods. They set off across the sands weighed down with iron - iron chariots, iron helmets and spears, iron shields, armour, the full works. As soon as the chariots start to get stuck in the sands, that's it. They climb down to pull the chariots and horses out and - with all that weight - well, the Celts were dead men before they even set foot in the sands."

"Jenny." Penny puts her head around the door and beckons me. It must be time to make the coffee

"As I was saying before, nothing has changed: the sands are still as dangerous. None of you must take he risk of walking out there alone. Many people have died as a result of underestimating the danger, and I don't want you to join them..."

"How's Dr Lune?" I ask Penny as we walk down the corridor towards the kitchen.

"Not so good. He'll have a terrible hangover to-morrow. He said he was going bird-watching as well with Marjorie."

"Is she still upstsairs with him?"

"Mmm. I told her to leave him to sleep it off but she prefers to kneel by his bedside and wipe his sweating brow."

"What a way to spend an evening!"

She shakes her head. "I'm appalled really. I mean, it's such an expensive school. Parents pay a fortune to send their sons there. I don't know what they'd say if they realized that their children were being looked after by a completely incompetent alcoholic and a silly woman who's totally besotted with him."

*   *   *

Dear Mum,
This is just a quick card to let you know that I've arrived all right. I've been busy cooking and serving behind the bar and looking after a crowd of lager louts from a posh private school. I'll tell you more about those later.

Some baby lambs have just been born and I'm looking forward to working on the farm.

I've got my own bedroom with a lovely view. I just can't get used to the owls hooting round at night.

I'll write more soon.
Lots of Love,
Jenny.
XXXXXXXX

I write my post card at the little wooden table in my bedroom, then I place it inside my shoulder bag ready for the post.

I look out of the window before I turn out the light. There's nothing there. Only darkness. At one time, I think I would have been afraid of so much blackness, looking out of my window and seeing nothing - no street lights, no house lights, no car headlights - all the things I'm used to. But there's something comforting about it. It's like the darkness when you close your eyes and go to sleep. Darkness of deep time, turning backwards and unfolding.

I still take my hot water bottle to bed. It isn't all that cold in my room but it's nice to have something to cuddle. I put the bottle inside my furry snowman cover, switch out the reading lamp and snuggle up. And it's then that I see the strange woman.

It's the woman I saw last night, with a white frilly cap, a long skirt and an apron. And she's standing in my room beside me, looking out of the window.

I feel afraid of what might happen now. I don't know what to think. I have been the same person all my life and now I am about to change. Things beyond my control. I don't know. I don't know what I shall do.

If it were at any other time of day, it would seem to be incredible. I know it's dark in my room and yet I can see her. I know she's standing by my bed but I feel sure that she can't see me. I don't feel afraid; I feel a kind of sympathy with her; she looks so young and worried.

I felt so pleased when he picked me out, so privileged. And then when he said how he would teach me reading – I who have always longed to read – and the books he gave me and the talks we had... He told me so many things. And I would sit with my mending and listen and build up the fire to keep us warm.

And now look what has become of this. He says I will be a lady, but I do not know. I may be able to read now but that doesn't turn a serving maid into a lady. I don't know if anything can.

Perhaps she only appears at bedtime. Or perhaps she's always there in my room, floating, talking to herself, staring out of my window. Perhaps it's only at this time of day that I can see her: the time between waking and falling asleep; the time between consciousness and dreaming

Eight

"Don't eat so much, Arnold. You can only have one seat on the coach going back, you know."

Arnold takes another sandwich from the pile. "This is only a snack," he explains.

"A snack!" Kent snorts. "Eight sandwiches, a pork pie, two packets of crisps and three Crunchy bars."

"If that's Arnold's snack," adds Warton, "I'd hate to see what his main course looks like."

"The coach door's only a metre wide, Arnold," says Kent. "We don't want you getting wedged."

"Imagine having Arnold instead of a coach door," Warton chuckles. "When we wanted some fresh air, we'd have to swing his legs up into the air."

I'm walking round the verandah before I go out to the field. I want to see how the baby lambs are getting on.

"Coming to say goodbye, Tulip?" Kent calls. When I turn round, he purses his lips as though he's expecting me to kiss him. "She'll miss us you know, chaps," he adds.

"Good job we'll be back again soon," says Arnold. "We don't want poor Tulip getting withdrawal symptoms."

I don't think there's much chance of that.

I wait until I see Arthur's coach careering down the drive before I go indoors. I've just time for a cup of tea and a muffin and then I have to start on my share of the clearing up.

The boys' rooms look like the aftermath of a hurricane in a garbage tip. There's rubbish everywhere. Not only

66

that, but there are muddy footprints where they've obviously clomped upstairs in their climbing boots and then, presumably, walked across the beds, the curtains, the easy chairs and the sinks. I don't know how people can be so ignorant. Part of my job is supposed to be emptying the rubbish bins, which would make sense if that's where the boys had left their rubbish, but they haven't. In some rooms, the waste paper bins are standing empty whilst all the rubbish is strewn about the floor. I open the windows to let in some fresh air and then I go downstairs and collect a pile of bin liners.

I always had the impression - and I realize now that this is probably stupid - that kids from rich homes were well-behaved. I thought pupils from private schools were always polite and did as they were told. I thought it was only kids in schools like ours who messed about. My mother always brought me up to think that rich people were cultured and well-educated. Now I know that it's possible to be wealthy and a lout.

I fill one bin liner with empty cans just from the first four bedrooms. I find bits of clothing like odd dirty socks and a pair of underpants. I bin those. I suppose I could find who slept in which room and send their filthy socks back to the school but I can't be bothered. I'm sure they won't even miss them.

The other thing that shocks me is the way their money's wasted. You see, where I live, if anyone buys a magazine, they always pass it on to someone else. If my mum buys Woman or Woman's Own, I'll always read them, then my gran, then she'll pass them to the lady next door who'll probably send them to the church jumble sale. If I ever buy any magazines, my mum'll read them, then I'll take them to school and they won't be thrown away until they've fallen to bits.

This lot have put brand new copies of *New Musical Express*, *Viz*, *Kerrang!* and *Gothic* straight in the bin. I bet lots of them haven't even been read once. I take them out and make a collection (of the more respectable ones, anyway) to keep in the library downstairs.

I carry the overflowing bin-liners down and stack them outside. My next job is to strip the beds and collect all the sheets and pillowcases together for the laundry. Then I have to fetch the trolley that's piled up with fresh clean sheets and pillowcases and scuttle through all the different rooms and make the beds. I used to think it was a drag to make my own bed; I never thought I might have to spend a Sunday afternoon making twenty seven others.

As I make the beds, Alli whizzes behind me with a hoover, sweeping up and polishing. I start three rooms ahead of her, but it's not long before she catches up. I think she's more used to hard work than I am. When we've done about half the rooms, we decide to take a tea break.

"Have you worked anywhere like this before, Jenny?" Alli asks me as she puts the kettle on.

"No. This is my first job."

"What do you think to it, then?"

Apart from the Belmount boys and all the hard work, it's wonderful. "I think I'm going to like it very much," I tell her.

Each corridor has a kitchen at the end with tea bags and coffee and mugs. Alli rinses out two mugs which contain dirty sweet wrappers, chewing gum, a page out of a Filofax and a ten pence piece as well as undrunk coffee. I look around for the tea towel.

"It's a bit unusual," Alli says. "I mean, it's not like working in a hotel."

The tea towel looks as though someone's used it for cleaning fifty pairs of climbing boots. I walk down to the linen trolley and fetch a clean one.

"The visitors aren't all as bad as this, are they?"

"No. The Belmount boys are the worst we have. The others are usually quite well behaved."

"It should be all right then, from now on."

"Well..." Alli pulls a face. "They'll be coming back in just over two months' time."

I sigh. I'd been hoping that Arnold was joking.

I think about the hill behind the house. I'm standing at the sink, up to my elbows in hot washing-up water, when I start to think about the rustic seat. I remember how it felt when I was sitting there. I remember its shadiness and dampness. I think about the garden. Going back to the Roots is the phrase that springs to my mind. I don't know why.

I take a scouring pad and scrub at the porridge which has stuck to the bottom of the pan. I have now learned that, no matter how dirty pans are, they will always come clean if only you scrub them hard enough.

Through the waves of soapy water, I can see the patterns of the wood mosaic. I can see the rusty nails, protruding from the bricks, quivering upwards like antennae.

I have also learned that it's best to stir the porridge all the time; then it never cakes together on the bottom. I never worried about that too much when my mum did most of the washing up.

Just around the corner from the seat is a kind of archway which leads inside the old brick wall. The creeper is everywhere; it blurs the edges of the buildings so it's hard to tell their shape, and the inside is overgrown with a forest of waist-high spindly trees.

I hesitate, because it all seems so unreal. It reminds me of a graveyard. I think about crumbling gravestones where plants push their way through concrete and stone. I can see that happening here. I can see the roots of plants sprouting through the walls, slowly breaking them apart and causing them to crumble.

I walk through the entrance in the old brick wall and the inside is like a sanctuary, a very quiet, sheltered place, surrounded by the ruins. The old wall is semi-circular and turretted around the top like the outside of a castle. I don't think it ever had a roof.

As I gaze around, I can make out more and more bits of buildings. Well, they're not buildings really, only their remains. Sections of walls and stones that are so covered in moss and leaves that you can hardly work out what they were. It's not a place where anyone would build a house because it's too steep and high up for that. It looks like a sort of arena. Perhaps it's the Celtic hill fort that Bernard was talking about.

I hesitate. I don't know whether to explore or not.

On my left is a low building, almost still intact. It reminds me of a coal bunker because it has a square low opening at the back as if that was where they used to shovel coal. I can't think why someone should have built a coal bunker up here. Especially the Ancient Celts. I decide to walk round and investigate.

There are four stone steps - old and smooth and almost covered with moss - which lead up to a platform and down again at the other side. I wonder if it might have been a theatre, a theatre in the open air. But I can't imagine who might have come here and what they would have come to watch.

70

I step cautiously on to the platform and gaze around. The sense of timelessness is very strong. It's because everything has softened. The moss and the creepers blur the outlines, so that objects seem less certain. It reminds me of the landscape after a heavy fall of snow. Everything that ought to be familiar is indistinct and curved; it's like something from a dream.

I think of a picture I saw once in a book in the art room at school. It was by a painter called Salvador Dali and it had watches and clocks sort of lying about flopping on the rocks by the side of the sea. That's just what it feels like here, as if time is somehow softening.

And that's when I hear the singing.

At first, it doesn't sound like singing; it's just a low, soft hum. I feel a shiver down my back. I can't see anyone about. I don't know where the humming's coming from because there's no one here but me.

My heart starts thudding like a drum machine. I tell myself not to be frightened. I look all about me, but all I can see are trees and ruins.

I begin to wonder if it might be someone passing with a Walkman, but the voice doesn't sound anything like a radio or a cassette recorder. And I know it's not the wind blowing through the trees because everything is still. The voice reminds me of the way my grandmother used to hum to herself when she was picking the black-currants in her garden.

Hm. Hmmmmm. Hm. Hmmmmm.

It just sounds like an old lady humming.

I can feel my arms coming out in goose pimples. I stare around the crumbling walls and the creepers, searching for the voice, but I can't see anyone there.

71

And that's when the singing starts. I don't know if it's a proper song or not; I don't think I've heard it before. It certainly isn't the kind of singing that you'd hear on Radio 1.

> *By night; by day;*
> *Alu La lay...*

And straightaway, I think about the strange woman in my room, the one who was standing by my bedside, staring through the window. I don't think it's her voice, but it's the same feeling I had when I saw her. A feeling of a kind of presence. Except that now I feel more scared. I feel as though this person's watching me and staring.

> *By night; by day;*
> *Alu La la*
> *Alu Rhiannon ...*

I swallow hard. I'm standing, frozen to the spot, but my eyes are looking round, searching everywhere. Round the top of the turreted wall, in between the branches of the trees, but I can't see anything. There doesn't seem to be any movement. I can't tell where the voice is coming from.

> *By night; by day;*
> *Alu La la*
> *Alu Rhiannon ...*

And then the voice stops. I still stand rigid, listening; I'm waiting for the sound of footsteps; I'm listening for the crackling of leaves. I'm waiting to see an old woman's face, peering over the turreted wall.

But I don't hear anything. Just the birds.

I wait a long time before I move. I feel scared to go back to the path and when I do, I creep forward very slowly, glancing round all the time.

I'm near the top of the hill where there's a bit of a clearing. It looks safer there. I climb to the summit and suddenly, there's a spectacular view. I can see the sea. Directly in front of me are the rest of the grounds of Castle Head. In the fields, I can see the scatterings of sheep, some of them with baby lambs and next to the fields is a golf course with people playing golf. I can see a tiny train, like a miniature railway and the train lines disappearing into the distance. Just off the coast is a little island.

I see all this in an instant, the view and the surroundings, but the only thing that really catches my attention is a solitary figure walking along the path. It's a woman walking on her own. An old woman. She looks a bit like a tramp with long grey hair and a sack across her shoulder and the bag seems to be weighing her down, so that one of her shoulders is much lower than the other. She's wearing a kind of shawl in gawdy colours - a mixture of purple, gold and red. I stare hard at the old woman and feel the goose pimples rising once more on my arms. I'm sure it's her. I swallow hard. I feel certain that she's the owner of the strange voice I heard, echoing round the walls. But if so, how did she get down there so quickly?

I feel the shivers again down my back.

Castle Head is haunted.

Nine

"What I enjoy about working here," says Alli as she makes us both a cup of tea, "is the variety. You see, you can work on the farm, you can go out canoeing with the children, you do a bit of cooking...you don't get bored. And the countryside's nice as well," she goes on. "There are lots of nice walks."

"Mmmm." I'm starting to feel less enthusiastic about the country walks. I open my mouth to start telling Alli all about the famous disembodied voice, but then I change my mind. I don't want her to think I'm a raving loony. "Do you ever go up to the top of the hill?" I ask her, pointing towards the back of the house.

"Mmm. We go there to put the bird boxes up." She passes me my mug. "There's a really nice view from the top. You can see right over the golf course and the railway line."

"I just wondered what those buildings were...you know, near the top...like ruins..."

"Oh, the walled garden."

I sit down and start to drink my tea. "Is that what it is? I thought it looked like a theatre."

"Mmmm. I suppose it does a bit. They say the priests built it." She passes me the biscuit tin. "Would you like a biscuit?"

"Thanks." I take a couple of chocolate bourbons. I could eat about eight actually, after all the hard work I've done today, but I don't want to seem too greedy.

"What priests?"

"Well, at one time, Castle Head was a kind of training centre for priests - the Holy Ghost Fathers. I think they were missionaries. They came here to train before they went to work abroad."

"I don't see why they should build a garden in such a funny place, though. I mean, there's all this flat land round about. Why would they build it on top of a hill?"

Alli shakes her head. "I don't know. I never thought really. Somebody just told me it was an enclosed garden. They said it was built on the same site as the ancient hill fort - I think that went right back to the Celts. They've found bits of jewellery and things.

"From thousands of years ago?"

"Mmm. That's right."

I drink my tea. "The priests didn't build this house though, did they?" I ask her.

"No." Alli reaches across for another biscuit. "The house was built by John Wilkinson. There's a big memorial to him in the village. It was erected in the garden originally, over his grave, but when the house was sold, people wanted it out of the way. I don't suppose anybody wanted to buy a house with a grave in the garden. I think it was right in front of the dining room windows."

I look out through the dining room windows when I go in to lay the table. I can't imagine where the gravestone could have been. I can't imagine either why anyone would want to be buried inside their own front garden. I always thought people had to be buried in churchyards if they didn't want to be cremated.

I draw the curtains and then I light the candles on the table. I open the doors of the dumb waiter and take out the bowls of horse radish sauce and the heated plates.

I'm starting to get into a routine now. I'm finding out what jobs need doing without having to be told. I know where things are kept. I'm learning what people expect of me as well.

Next week there'll be some younger children staying at Castle Head. I think I'll find it easier to work with them because they'll think of me as a grown up and expect me to tell them what to do. I don't think they'll be rude or make fun of me or anything. Perhaps next week things will settle down.

Thank goodness tomorrow's my day off.

Ten

The village lies in the opposite direction from the station. It isn't very far away. It has a pub and a post office and several rows of cottages and a big monument to John Wilkinson. It says how the monument was moved from Castle Head but it doesn't explain why. There's the sound of water everywhere because there are streams rushing down from the hills - one of them appears from underground at the side of the street, flows into a horse trough and then out and underneath the road. There are a few expensive-looking houses but there are lots more tiny cottages with names like Nutwood and Hazelwood with tiny little garden paths and gates. It reminds me of the feeling I had when I first arrived, as if everything's unreal, like a kind of toytown in a children's story book.

I post the postcard to my mum, then, up a winding lane, I see the churchyard. The church itself lies in a strange position because it's in a kind of dell. I always expect churches to stand high up on a hill where you can see them, but this one's sheltered in a hollow. The hill, in fact, is behind the church.

I'm hoping to look inside the church because there are things I want to find out. There's a special reason for my coming to this part of the world apart from the fact that it was the only place that I could get a job. I'm still hoping that I might be able to find out something about my proper mother.

I open the green wrought-iron gate and walk down the stone steps that lead towards the graveyard. It's very quiet. Some of the graves are tidy and well-cared for and others are falling apart and overgrown with ivy. There are clumps of daffodils in flower and a rockery that's filled with purple heather, but other parts of the graveyard look a bit neglected. By the side of the church, for instance, is a large flat grave with the stone slab on top all broken up. It looks as though, if someone pushed you over, you'd just fall inside with all the skeletons.

Beside the church porch is something very unusual: a narrow flight of stone steps leading downwards. Of course, I go down to explore them because that's the kind of person I am - I always like exploring. At the bottom, instead of a room (or the secret passage I was really hoping to find), there's part of a stream. It's really strange - just an underground stream with this flight of steps leading down into it. I can only imagine that, in the olden days when people didn't have proper plumbing, they used to walk down here with buckets to fetch their water.

The door to the church is unlocked, so I decide to go inside. My plan is to go round all the churchyards in the area. Then I can check out the names on the gravestones. The church is nice and warm. I walk round looking at the different names on the stained glass windows and on the memorial stones. It's a lovely old church and I feel very relaxed. I don't feel scared or anything because I'm on my own or because the grave-yard is outside. I just wander round by myself, taking it all in.

At the front of the church, by the side of a carved wooden pulpit, are a couple of things relating to Castle Head. First of all, there's a memorial stone.

It says:

SACRED
TO THE MEMORY OF
MARY WILKINSON
WIFE OF
JOHN WILKINSON ESQ OF CASTLEHEAD
IRONMASTER
WHO DIED DECEMBER X1X, MDCCCVI
AGED LXXXIII
SHE WAS HUMBLE, LIBERAL AND BELOVED.

I don't know what the Roman numbers mean. I try to
work them out but I get stuck. It seems an unusual way
to describe someone who's died. It makes me start to
wonder what anyone might say about me.

HERE LIES JENNY BROWN
WHO WASN'T VERY GOOD AT SCHOOL
AND HAD A PASSION FOR HOT BUTTERED
MUFFINS AND MILK SHAKE.

That's the only interesting thing about me I can think of.
Next to the memorial is a stained glass window. The
main figure in it is a woman with a halo. Underneath, it
says:

CHARITY

But it doesn't say which charity it's supposed to be.
Below that, it says:

To the Glory of God and in Loving Memory of
Jane (Jenny)

and something about Edward Mucklow of Castle Head

and his wife, Deborah.

Behind the Charity lady is a lovely sunset and perched right on top of the window is a badger. A picture of one, that is - not a real one. I find that amusing because I never realized there was anything holy about badgers. I mean, I don't think they're even mentioned in the Bible. Perhaps the person who painted the window was just very fond of badgers and wanted to put one in.

I'm just thinking about that - looking at the badger and wondering why it's there, when suddenly I feel really frightened. There's somebody staring at me. Well, when I say somebody, I can't actually see their body at all; all I can see are their eyes. I feel the hair stand up on the back of my arm the way it does when I watch a scary video.

But this is not a video.

Next to the stained glass window is another one made of plain glass. It has a red border round the edge and the glass inside the border is opaque - you can't see through it at all. But that's not where the eyes are. There are tiny panes of transparent glass between the red border and the edge of the window and that's where the eyes are. Staring. The gap is too small for me to see the whole face but I feel sure that it's an old woman, a very old woman. I can just make out her straggly grey hair.

Sraightaway, I think about the old woman at Castle Head, the one I heard humming in the garden. I feel sure it's her. She must be following me. Her eyes are staring straight at me. I don't move at all; I just stand and gape at her with my mouth open. You see, the window is too high for anyone to be standing on the ground; it's as if the face - the woman - is suspended in the air; that's why I think perhaps it has to be a ghost.

I close my eyes for a second, to make sure I'm not just

dreaming, and when I open them again, the face has gone. I look all round me. I feel cold and shivery. My arms are tingling with goose pimples even though the church is nice and warm. I feel frightened. I listen for any sound of movement. I listen for any humming. I strain my ears and listen for the croaky voice, a-lu-la-laying round the gravestones. But everything is silent. If the door opened now and the vicar walked in, I'd probably have a heart attack.

I look at all the other windows and then turn and glance behind me. I don't want to see her again. I don't know what to do. I feel as if I'm being haunted.

I decide to go outside. I feel scared that the old woman might come inside the church and look for me. I think I'll feel safer in the graveyard.

I open the door of the church and peer outside, but there's no one there. On my right is the flight of stone steps leading downwards to the stream, but she can't have gone down there; she can't have floated away in the water.

I walk down the pathway in the graveyard as far as the Charity window. In front of it, there's a large, flat-topped tomb. Someone could have stood on there and peered in through the stained glass. But that's the wrong window, of course. The next window is the plain one, the one where I saw the eyes and all that has below it is the tomb with the cracked and crumbling lid. If someone had stood on the broken tomb, then they might have been able to peer in through the window, but it looks too dangerous to stand on. And why would anyone do that anyway? If they wanted to look at the church, why didn't they walk inside like I did? And where are they now? I walk gingerly over to the tomb with the cracks and have a peep inside it, but I'm sure there's no one there.

I glance up and down the graveyard, but it's empty. Apart from me and all the dead bodies. I have a horrible feeling that the old woman is hiding somewhere, watching me. I imagine her peering out at me from behind one of the crumbling gravestones. I shudder. I think I'll go back to Castle Head. I feel disappointed because there are some seats in front of the daffodils where I could have had a sit down.

Anyway, it's turning cooler now. I button up my jacket. There are dark clouds in the sky and I don't want to get caught in the rain again. I decide to set off back to Castle Head.

Eleven

Castle Head Field Studies Centre
Grange over Sands
Cumbria

Monday

Dear Mum
*I'm still enjoying myself very much although
they've been keeping me very busy, so I'm afraid
that's why you haven't had all the long letters from
me that I promised.*

*I've been cleaning and cooking and looking after
some little primary school children and helping on
the farm. My favourite job is feeding the baby
lambs. I've helped to look after six of them so far
and all of them are doing well - sorry, all except
one. There's a little black lamb called Sooty who
seems to be blind but I think the others will be all
right.*

*The weather has been quite good so I've been for
lots of walks on my days off.*

*The other people here are very nice. The main
person I work with is called Alli. She's a lot older
than me but it doesn't matter because we get on
quite well together.*

*I don't know if you remember my mentioning this
before, but I did think I would like to try to find out
about my real mother. I nearly wrote "proper
mother" but, of course, you will always be my*

*proper mum. I just feel very curious about it all
and would like to know who she is. I know you said
that she once worked at a hotel around here, and I
wondered if you could remember anything else.
Can't you remember which hotel it was, for
instance? I've looked in two of the churchyards but
I can't see the name anywhere.*

*Anyway, I'm hoping to come back home at the
weekend for your birthday. This will be my first
whole weekend off so it should be nice. Don't
worry, I won't be bringing my dirty washing. I've
been able to do that here.*

I'll give you a ring later in the week.

Lots of love,

Jenny
xxxxxxx

It'll be good to see my mum again. I'll have to buy her a
present for her birthday. I don't know what. I think
about it as I lie in bed, wondering what she might like.
And it's then that I hear the voice again, the voice of the
young girl. It's almost as if she's thinking aloud, but her
thoughts are sounding loud inside my head just as if I'm
the one that's thinking them.

That's how he was. That's how he was when he told
me. Sitting by the fireside, with his head down deep
inside his hands, staring at the floor. That's how he was.
And I, not knowing what else I should do, could only sit
and listen. Mending my stockings by the fireside when
my reading book had been laid down. "You know,
Anne, I have never once fathered a son," he told me. "I
have no heir to my estate."

I nodded and spoke nothing because all that was common knowledge. We knew our master had no son and we knew how his nephew, Thomas, would inherit. We had talked about it often times in the past, grouped round the kitchen table, speculating on the changes that the younger man would make. Thinking how it would be to have a younger man in charge. "Perhaps Master Thomas would have a grand house in London," Mary said, "and all of us should be in service there."

We laughed aloud at that and thought on it and considered what changes it would make. But now my life is going to change in ways I can't consider, ways I cannot know.

And after prayer time in the evening, I say a prayer myself now. I pray that one day I shall bear a son, because I know how strongly that is what he wants. And I know also that the conceiving of a son is the touchstone of my fortune or my undoing. That is why I keep the ancient ring of serpents. My good luck charm. That it will be that makes my fortune.

Later in the week, I have some more free time. "You do realize you're just being spoiled," Penny says, "because it's your first week. "

I give a sheepish grin.

"You'll have to make it all up later on, you know," says Alli. "You'll be working sixteen hours a day, scrubbing the floors, cleaning out the toilets..."

"...shearing the sheep..."

I hope they're joking.

"Are you going out for a walk, then?" Alli asks when she passes me in the hallway with my coat on.

"I thought I'd walk down into Grange. I want to buy some postcards," I explain. "And a bird book."

"Well you've picked a nice day for it."

I got up too late for breakfast so I decide to have elevenses in one of the little cafés opposite the station. There's a nice row of shops there, with chairs and tables outside facing the ornamental gardens. I'm spoiled for choice because there's the Chocolate Shop, the Hazelmere and The Cedar Tree Café. In the end, I decide on the Hazelmere. I walk inside and order a strawberry milk shake. They sell lots of home-made cakes; in fact, the counter is packed with treacle tarts, egg custards, caramel squares and coconut slices. They look really appetizing, but I decide to just have a buttered muffin. That's partly because the prices here are about as high as the Travellers Fayre in Preston and I don't have that much money, but also the food is so good at Castle Head, and it's free, that it seems a waste to buy food from anywhere else.

I sit down with my milk shake and take out the paper bag with the things I've bought at the station: my bird book and the postcards. My mum's card has a picture of the ornamental gardens with a little girl feeding the ducks. I think she'll like that.

It's a beautiful day and I walk along by the side of the beach. The sun is glistening on the few pools of water left by the tide but, apart from that, the sands are vast and smooth as a desert. Except, that on the horizon I can see what seems to be a power station. Looking back, there's the railway line and the prom-enade and, in the distance, the grey hills of the southern Lake District.

After a while, I walk down a country lane which runs parallel with the sea. There are lovely cottages with orchards and flowers everywhere. I notice one house, on the corner with a huge magnolia tree in the garden. It's just coming into flower.

Along the lane is a very old white house with tiny windows. It has ornaments in the front garden and hens at the side. In front of the house is a notice:

CEDRIC ROBINSON
GUIDES FARM, CARTER LANE
For walks, talks, books on Morecambe Bay.

That must be the Cedric that Bernard was talking about. The one who shows people the way across the sands.

A few metres further on is a seat by the side of the wall. I sit down and look through the bird book. I've seen some big ducks out on the sands and I'm wondering what they are. They're sort of orange and black and white striped. According to the book, they might be Shelducks. *Sociable bird, usually seen feeding on mud or sand flats* it says. That sounds favourite. I'll have to get a bit closer to make sure.

Before I go, I notice something unusual. All the cottages have gardens which are well cared-for and tidy. Their hedges are trim and neat, but just next to me is the untidiest hedge I've ever seen. It's overgrown with spindly branches waving into the air like the arms of people at a pop concert. It's a shrub people don't normally have for a hedge. I recognize it straightaway, because my gran has a bush of it in her garden. The leaves are pointed and shiny and mottled. When the sun shines on them they look varnished, sort of lacquered and polished. It's called laurel; a hedge of laurel. I remember Bernard saying something about laurel when he gave his talk. Something to do with Cedric but I can't remember what.

I'm sitting in the sunshine, enjoying the peace and quiet with only the birds making any sound at all, when suddenly a motor starts up. It's like a great big saw. It makes a noise worse than a dentist's drill.

I look around but I can't see anything happening. There doesn't seem to be anyone about. The sawing seems to be coming from the back garden of the farm beside me. I think it's a chain saw. It's probably Cedric Robinson. He must have bought the chain saw to cut his hedge; it's about time somebody gave it a trim.

I walk along to the end of the lane. On my left is a wall of white stones, held together by a mass of tiny purple flowers. I don't know what they are. Maybe I'll have to buy a book of wild flowers next.

I ease my way through a swinging iron gate. The top rail is worn as smooth as marble, but the rest of the gate is rusty. All around me is the scent of wild flowers.

After a while, the path comes down to another little railway station. KENT SANDS. It reminds me of Kent Wilkinson. I cross over the railway line and pass through another swinging gate. Then I'm on the beach. I stand for a few minutes, just to enjoy the view.

I know I'll have to start making my way back now. I've walked a very long way; a bit of exercise is reasonable but I don't want to finish up exhausted. This is supposed to be my day off.

On one of the rocks beside me is a notice:

CUMBRIA COUNTY COUNCIL
WARNING

The right of way across the bay to Hest Bank crosses dangerous sands. Do not attempt to cross without the official guide.

T.J.R. Whitfield
clerk and chief executive

Guide: Mr C. Robinson, Guides Farm, Cart Lane, Grange over Sands.

Well, if anybody goes to knock up the official guide today, he won't be able to hear them. He's too busy sawing up his laurels.

Anyway, I don't know where Hest Bank is and I'm certainly not thinking of trekking across the bay. All I want to do is walk back on the edge of the beach.

I set off but it doesn't take me long to decide that, if people come to Grange to have a nice relaxing holiday on the sands, they ought to get their money back. This isn't sand; it's mud. Miles and miles of mud. Of course, I haven't brought my wellies; I'm only wearing my little ankle boots. The surface of the mud is smooth but then, as you put your weight down, there's a kind of sucking; I can feel my boot being pulled away from my heel with every step I take. I daren't walk too quickly, because the mud is so slippery on the surface that I keep sliding about. I don't want to fall down in it. I can just imagine what I'd look like, strolling back past all the dainty tea shops, caked in mud from head to toe. The mad swamp woman of Grange over Sands. I decide to head towards the rocks.

I try dipping my feet in some of the little pools to clean my boots, but the mud is so sticky it's like trying to wash away black treacle. My boots must weigh twice as much as they did before. I'll have to find some grass to wipe them on. I stumble across the rocks. They're not easy to walk on either; they're shaped like giant sponges. They remind me of the photographs in our school geography book of the lava flow from a volcano. When I see another path leading back across the railway line, I make my way towards it.

I wipe my boots on the grass and check out the ducks again. I'm pretty certain that they're shelducks. I've only got about another five hundred sorts of birds to learn and I can consider myself an expert.

The path leads back to Carter Lane, but my way is blocked by a van with Cumbrian TV written on the side. I bet it's the same one that drove straight past me in the rain. The driver seems to be whizzing round in circles. I have to stand and wait because I don't know where they're going next. There isn't any pavement, the lane is very narrow and I'm in great danger of being completely flattened. It would be a lot safer walking on the railway line.

I stand and watch for a few moments, intrigued, and then the man in the passenger seat sees me and starts to wave. He looks like an escaped lunatic. I'm just about to run away, when he winds down his window and beckons me, pointing to a map. I sigh and walk across.

"I wonder if you could, er...we seem to have er..."

He's a middle-aged chap with long blond hair combed forward in a sixties Beatle-style. I think it must be a wig.

"I wonder if you know where the...er..."

He's wearing a fur-lined, leather flying jacket (this is a warm, sunny day, remember) and a flowered silk cravat. He also has a gold earring, just one.

Just then the driver leans across. She's a young, slim, black woman - very glamorous with fancy-framed glasses and polished fingernails. "Could you tell us where Guide's Farm is?" she asks politely.

She seems more normal. I'm just about to give her directions when the lunatic interrupts. "We're looking for C..e..d..r..i..c R..o..b..i..n..s..o..n." He sounds out the words as though I'm only six years old, as though I'm deaf and as though I'm completely stupid. "C..e..d..r..i..c. R..o..b..i..n..s..o..n.."

I point to the large white cottage at the bottom of the lane. I feel very tempted to sound out the words to him, the way he spoke to me, but I'm too polite. "It's down there," I tell him. I hope he doesn't think Cedric will take them skating across the bay in the Cumbrian TV van. It'd be sucked straight into the sands like an earwig in a vat of chocolate.

"That's super, darling. Absolutely super," says the maniac in the Beatle-wig. "That's incredibly helpful."

He turns to the driver. "Have you got that, Cartmel? It's over there."

Cartmel raises her eyebrows at me but says nothing. I bet he sends her completely round the bend. I hope she's not his wife.

The idiot holds up his hand and gives me a babyish wave, like a children's puppet, moving only his fingers, as Cartmel negotiates an eight-point turn in the middle of the lane.

Twelve

When I went home a few weekends ago, I took a present for my mum. It wasn't anything very expensive. It was a little basket with soap and bath oil and things, all made in the Lake District and all of them in pine. She seemed very pleased with it. She always says, "Oh you shouldn't have, Jenny. You know you shouldn't. You don't get very much money."

But if I didn't buy her anything, I'm sure she'd be disappointed. It just occurs to me how nice it is to have a mum that's so easy to please. It occurs to me as well, because I've been thinking about the boys from Belmount School, that how ever much money their parents might spend on them, they'll never be really grateful. I don't think they'd ever appreciate things that anyone does for them.

I go outside for a bit of a walk. I like to watch the sunset and I like to hear the birds.

When I went back home, it was good to see my mum again and I really enjoyed telling her what I've been doing, but there was something I found a bit sad, as well. I feel as though my mum and I are growing further apart.

The main reason is that my mother's changing. She started to change, or I first noticed it anyway, after my dad left home. At first, I felt worried about her because she always used to look so sad. I used to make a special effort to be helpful, cooking meals sometimes and bringing her cups of tea and doing the ironing. A lot of the time, though, she just sat staring out of the window or watching the tv; she didn't seem to really take much notice of what was going on.

After a year or so, she became very different. She went on a slimming campaign, and had her hair cut shorter. Then she bought a leotard and joined a keep-fit class and started to learn word-processing. After that, she got a job as a secretary at the children's hospital. I was very pleased for her. It was good to see her looking brighter. But, only a short while after that, she started going out with men.

She'd never been out with men before - not that I knew of anyway, - only my dad - and now here she was going out drinking, eating meals in restaurants and not coming home till late. I didn't know what to think. She hadn't even waited till she'd got divorced.

One reason why I felt a bit spare was because I was the teenager - I was the one who was supposed to be going out on dates and things and, of course, I didn't have a boyfriend. I sat at home with Gary Glitter the goldfish and the kitten whilst my mother was discoing the night away. That seemed a bit embarrassing.

I also felt as though, quite suddenly, my mum didn't want me around any more; she wanted to get on with her own life. When I was younger, I'd felt very close to her, but now I was growing up I felt as though she just wanted me out of the way.

I'm not saying this in a nasty way because I love my mother very much and she's always been nice to me, but it made me start thinking more about my real mum, wondering who she was.

This started when my dad left home because, one of the things I kept thinking about at that time was the fact that my parents had told me I was adopted. When my dad went off and left us, it seemed less painful if I kept reminding myself that he'd never been my real father anyway.

I first found out that I was adopted when we were doing family trees at school. Our new teacher, Miss Conyers, told us how we were going to trace our family back. She explained how to draw the family tree and told us to ask our parents for the correct names of our grandparents and great grandparents.

I remember the expression on my mum's face when I asked her. She looked down at the table, first of all. Then, after a pause, she sort of raised her eyebrows at my dad. I glanced across at him. He didn't say anything at all, but he nodded.

"Our parents are not your real grandparents," my mum explained. "That's because you've been adopted. Have you ever heard that word before?"

I shook my head.

"Well, sometimes there are babies whose parents can't look after them properly," she explained. "Their parents might be very ill or they might have died. Their babies go to be adopted."

"Like in an orphanage?" I asked her.

"That's right."

"It isn't anything to be ashamed of, Jenny," my father said.

I never thought it was.

"Well, when we found that we weren't able to have any children, we went to an adoption agency."

"And is that where you got me from?" I asked her.

"That's right."

I thought it was quite a nice idea. I had this picture of them going to an orphanage and looking at the rows of children whose parents had died and then deciding I was the nicest baby there.

I learned later on that it wasn't quite like that. I learned that my mother was unmarried, which meant that my real father might not even know of my existence.

After my other father left home, I used to daydream. I had this idea that my real father might be rich and famous - a pop singer perhaps or a film star. I thought that maybe his wife had never been able to have any children and, when I wrote to him, he would send a big chauffeur-driven car to fetch me. I'd arrive at the film or tv studios where he was working and then he'd introduce me to everyone: "Look, everyone," he'd say. "This is my daughter, Jenny. Isn't she wonderful?"

There would be photographs of us in the papers, side by side: Pop Star Unites With Long-Lost Daughter and he'd shower me with presents. I don't like to think I wanted the presents just because I was greedy, but because it would show how much he cared for me.

I walk along by the side of the river. The fish are jumping out of the water. I hear a splash and then see the circles of ripples. Sometimes, if I'm just looking in the right place, I see a little flash of silver as the fish leaps out. I like to stand and stare, because that's the only way to see the fish. By the time you hear the splash, they've gone under the water again.

When I went home, it was my mum's birthday and, what I hadn't realized was that her new boyfriend had arranged to take her out on Saturday night. I didn't mind, of course. I mean, it would be awful if she was just sitting at home on her own all the time.

My mum asked me if I would like to join them. "We can change the booking for three," she explained. "I'm sure there'll be plenty of room."

"No, that's all right," I told her. "I'll stay here and

watch tv."

"I thought there might be some of your old friends you might have wanted to look up."

I'd thought about that already, but there wasn't anyone I wanted to see. I felt quite happy staying in and watching telly.

I always like to walk round the grounds in the early evening. The daffodils have faded now and withered and we have bluebells instead, rising like a soft blue mist amongst the trees.

The first lambs are starting to be weaned now. They wander away from the ewes and nibble at clumps of fresh grass. We still feed the weak lambs with bottled milk but only three times a day instead of four.

Over the past few weeks, we've had a lot of young people staying here and they've all been well behaved. Even their rooms have been tidy. We've had groups of older students from a university and a polytechnic and some adults who hardly needed any looking after at all. The little children who stayed here called me Auntie Jenny and they kept coming and asking if there were any jobs they could do. When I let them help me feed the lambs they were really thrilled. I can just imagine what Kent and Arnold would say if I asked them to help me set the table or clean out the goats.

I talked to my mum about it when I went home for the weekend, but she wasn't much help. "Tell Mr Wharf," she said, "if they're out of order. It's not your job to teach them how to behave."

Mr Wharf is Bernard and I don't really want to run to him. That's partly because it would make me feel like a snitch at school but also, because I don't want him and Penny to get the impression I can't cope. I haven't done anything else much wrong - not since the tulip ratatouille - and I like it so much at Castle Head, in spite of all the ghosts, that I really do want to stay.

You see, I'm still not permanently employed. I don't mean that I'm on a training scheme - it is a proper job, but it's just on a temporary basis for the first few months. "That'll give us a chance to get to know each other," Bernard said at my interview. "See whether you think this is the kind of environment you want to work in or not. And see whether we think you're suitable."

At first I was afraid of them sacking me mainly because it would mean going back home to the dole queue. But now there's something else as well. Now that I've been home and seen how much my mum has changed, I know I wouldn't feel really welcome if I went back to live with her again. I'm starting to think of my home as being here at Castle Head. If they were to sack me now, I wouldn't have anywhere else to live.

Thirteen

"Are you coming in to watch the rushes, Humphrey?"

No answer.

Watching the rushes of the last few days' shooting is one of the jobs that Humphrey normally enjoys. It's work he can do sitting back in a comfy chair, with a cigar and a glass of French brandy - a situation in which he feels more at home than shivering on a wind-swept beach.

Today, he is putting it off. He collects his papers together, pats his head and curls up in embarrassment.

"There's some brandy here for you."

"Would you like ice, Humphrey?"

Lin Dale and Cartmel sit next to each other beside the video. Cartmel has a glass of fresh orange juice. Lin, who still feels chilly after spending six hours out in the driving wind and rain, has a mug of minestrone soup.

"We're all ready, Humphrey."

"Is there anything wrong?"

Lin and Cartmel both know what is wrong, but humouring Humphrey Head has become a way of life to them. After all, he is their boss.

Humphrey drinks a whole glass of brandy at once. Then he pours himself another generous portion before he sits down to watch the video.

"Have you got your script, Humphrey?"

Humphrey looks at his secretary as though he doesn't even know what the word means."

"Here you are."

Shifting Sands - Morecambe Bay - Take One.

...When the tide is out, the sands of Morecambe Bay look deceptively safe. Throughout the centuries many travellers have crossed the Sands rather than make the twenty mile detour...

Humphrey sits back in his chair taking long, deep breaths. He wishes he could find it easy to relax.

On many occasions in the past, coaches had to be abandoned when they went down in the soft sands and passengers were lucky to escape...

He tries to remember some of the techniques his therapist, Harvey, used to teach him. Start by relaxing the little toe on the left foot. Push it out, make it tense, then let it float gently down inside the carpet. Then start on the next toe...Humphrey slips off his shoe to make the process easier.

In 1808, a group of coffin-bearers got into difficulties. They were carrying the iron coffin of John Wilkinson, a local ironmaster, when their coach overturned and the coffin sank into the sand. The coffin, fortunately, was recovered when the tide went out...

Humphrey shakes his head. "Well, that's a lesson to us all not to be buried in an iron coffin. Right. What have we got next? The dead bodies?"

The churches around the bay all have registers containing details of people drowned in their attempts to cross the Sands. For example, William Stout of Lancaster wrote in 1687...

Now move on to the right foot. Feel as though each toe is floating away...floating, floating...

Humphrey takes off his right shoe and wiggles around to make himself more comfortable.

Concentrate on weightlessness. Allow your feet to feel abandoned. Let them float away...

"Oh dear. Help! I think I'm falling into the quicksands!"

Humphrey cringes at the video. "You look a complete twerp there, Lin."

Lin says nothing.

"I mean, if you'd just moved around a bit. Tried to make it seem as if you were struggling. You look as if you've just stepped into a baby's sand pit."

"Would you like another drink, Humphrey?"

Humphrey passes his glass across for Cartmel to fill.

"But I really was going down," Lin tries to explain for the eighteenth time.

"I mean, those shots are absolutely useless. I showed you how to do it in the studio."

Cartmel turns her head to avoid Lin's eyes as she remembers Humphrey's famous performance, sinking into the studio carpet, waving like Andy Pandy.

"But the sands were sucking on my feet. I could have been drowned."

Humphrey drinks some more brandy and looks back at the video.

"Help! I'm falling into the....Look, Humphrey, you BLEEP twerp. Will you BLEEP well get me out of here. I'm going to BLEEP drown in a minute."

"Okay, point taken. Cue the old whirlybird."

Whirring of helicopter blades.

"You should have listened to Cedric Robinson. He told you it was dangerous. They're never going to BLEEP well get me out. Where's that BLEEP helicopter?"

"It's all right, darling. You're being rescued now."

"I'm just going further into the BLEEP sands."

"Don't panic, you'll be all right. Now, try to wave your arms the way I showed you."

"BLEEP OFF!"

Humphrey sits back on his easy chair and inhales on his cigar. He tries to remember how to relax his left toe, then decides he might do it better after another glass of brandy.

He watches as the video degenerates into a state of total confusion. First of all, as the helicopter approaches, the wind from its propellers wafts all the pages of his script across the mudflats. Lin Dale, now up to her calves in sand, is shrieking words of abuse that make even the film crew's ears turn scarlet. Fortunately, some of her worst expletives are drowned in the whirring of propeller blades. And then finally, the scene that Humphrey has been dreading: as the helicopter dips lower and lower to rescue Lin, the crew are surrounded by what seems like a small tornado. As the helicopter whirls over Humphrey, the wind from its propellers whisks up his famous hairpiece. There is a close-up of Humphrey, bald as a pink balloon, waving to the pilot to forget about Lin and concentrate on recovering his blond Beatle wig, before it is blown away across the mudflats to be buried forever in the quicksands.

Humphrey strokes his denuded scalp. "Pour me another brandy, Cartmel," he sighs. "You know, I think we'll have to shoot this scene again."

Fourteen

"Here we go! Here we go! Here we go!"

I'm just finishing cleaning round the bath when my ears are ruptured by what most people would assume to be an invasion of football hooligans.

"Here we go! Here we go! Here we go-o..."

I squeeze a dollop of Jiff on to my cloth and try to erase the tide mark left by twenty five eight year olds who seem to have all been having a bath together.

"When we meet again, we'll eat again tulips from Amsterdam!"

I tiptoe across the room and push the bolt home on the door. I want to keep my privacy as long as possible.

"Now we're here again, we'll fear again tulips from Amsterdam!"

I rub as hard as I can on the tidemark and then rinse the bath round with cold water. I ought to be downstairs really with Alli, helping to allocate the rooms.

I wring out my cloth and, as I'm waiting for the cold water to gurgle down the plughole, I look out of the window at the jackdaws.

I always open the bathroom windows when I clean in here because the smell from the toilets is not too pleasant, and that's how I came to find out about the jackdaws. Castle Head is built on different levels, and this window opens on to the roof below; across it, I can see the clock tower where the jackdaws nest. A few weeks ago I would have just said that they were big black birds.

Often to be seen strutting on ground and rooftops, it

103

says in my birdbook. *Nests in buildings, cliff-faces and trees.*

These have built a nest in the old clock tower. That might explain why the clocks have stopped at different times: it's always half past seven on one clock and quarter to four on the other.

"Here we go! Here we go! Here we go!"

I close the window and tidy my cleaning things away. Then there's the sound of footsteps in the corridor behind the bathroom door.

"Here we are, Doctor."

"Right-i-ho."

"Should be well away from the Infidel up here."

"Jolly well hope so. Can't do with that lot up here."

"Specially when we're bird-watching!"

This last statement produces huge guffaws of laughter from Marjorie and the doctor. They have a very strange sense of humour.

"Let's get the cases in then straight down to the bar, eh what?"

"And I suppose yours'll be a pint of lager!"

At the mention of the pint of lager, they both seem to collapse again into hysterics. I don't know what's the matter with them.

Anyway, it's no use my standing here day-dreaming with my floor-cloth and my Jiff. I have to go down and face what some people might call music.

"Are we all off to the pub tonight then?"

"Certainly are old chap."

"Get a few extra calories down you, eh, Arnold? Don't want you wasting away."

"If Arnold's wasting away, I'd hate to see what a fat chap looks like."

They're lounging around the library now, watching me mend the fire. I think they'd have sat and watched it go out rather than have the initiative to throw a couple of extra logs on.

"You coming too then, Kent?"

"Actually, no."

"No?"

"What's this, Kent? On an alcohol-free diet, are we?"

"No. Got a bit of an awkward situation, Warton."

"What's that?"

"Expecting a visit from the old man."

I stand some more logs at the side of the fireplace. I don't know whether to explain that, if the fire dies down in future, it would be a good idea to put some more wood on. I don't know how they can be so stupid.

"Oh, is this the great birthday present?"

"What have you asked him for, Kent? A yacht?"

"A holiday in the Bahamas?"

Kent shakes his head. "I was hoping for a jetski, but there's been a bit of a cock-up..."

"Would have been all right though, wouldn't it? Wizz across to Morecambe on that on Friday night..."

"What's the cock-up, Kent? Your old man forgotten your birthday?"

"Probably not the most exciting day of his life, hey? The day little baby Kent appeared."

"Can you just imagine him in his Babygro."

"With his feeding bottle!"

"He'd probably have it filled with lager!"

They all laugh at this. They seem to think they're really funny. I just sweep the mess out of the hearth. Then I walk across and draw the curtains.

"Last week everything was hunky dory. Wrote home to the folks. Told them everything was fine. Said how

hard I was working, excellent marks. All my assignments done. Exams looking very hopeful. Portfolio fine
on the old stock market. Opening a deposit account in
the building society..."

"Weren't they impressed then?"

"I wrote another letter on the same day."

"That sounds a bit energetic for you, Kent."

"You'd need a long rest after that."

"Mmm, well. I wrote to my cousin, Henry. Told him
the real story. How the bank manager called me in and
I'd had to sell all the stocks and shares. How I'd not
done any assignments yet this term. Exam prospects nil.
Spent most of the term in bed with a hangover, you
know the sort of thing..."

"Sounds more like you, Kent."

"So, what was wrong?"

"Well, I put the letters in the wrong envelopes. Posted
the folks' letter to cousin Henry and Henry's letter to the
folks."

"Oh no!"

I can't help smiling to myself at this. It serves him
right.

"My old man faxed straight through to the school.
Says it's high time he and I had a serious chat."

"Sounds like bad news, Kent."

"So he's coming to see me tonight. And I've got an
unpleasant feeling that he'll be leaving my jetski
behind."

Fifteen

"Barmaid in here by any chance?"

I'm not too keen on being called a barmaid, but I look up from sweeping down the hearth.

"Could we have some drinks, please, dear?"

Fortunately, Penny happens to be walking past. "It's all right, Jenny," she tells me, "I'll see to the teachers' drinks. Perhaps you could go and feed the lambs. It's nearly time for them to have their bottles."

I escape from the house with six bottles of warm milk clasped inside my coat. I run down the path towards the farm as the evening sky is starting to turn red. I open the gate and fasten it behind me as I walk into the trampled mud of the farmyard. And a heron wings past me towards the river. I don't need to look up herons in my bird book now; I see them all the time. They're huge and slate grey with legs like pairs of bent drinking straws and they always land at the water's edge.

I've fallen in love with the farm. I even love the mud and the smell of goats. I feel at home here. I think I'll always remember it, even when I'm old: this farmyard in the stillness of the evening with the baby goats and the lambs, and me, standing here and feeding them with an occasional heron flying past. I don't want anything else. If life was just like this from now on, I'd be happy.

As I walk back towards Castle Head, Dr Lune and Marjorie are strolling down the path from the back door. They look around, as if they're uncertain about which way to go.

"Can I help you?" I ask.

"Well..." Marjorie seems to be standing very close to the doctor, nudging him as she struggles to stifle a giggle. "We were....we were going to do some bird-watching," she chuckles.

It seems a bit late for bird-watching to me. It'll be getting dark soon. "If you go over there..." I point towards the river, "...you'll probably see a heron. It'll be standing by the water's edge."

"Thank you very much," says the Doctor. "We'll go down to the river and see the heron then, shall we Marjorie?"

I'm surprised they haven't got a pair of binoculars or even a bird book between them. I suppose I could offer to lend them mine. They walk off in the direction of the woods. I don't know how they think they can spot any birds in there when it's starting to get dark.

I walk back towards the house as the biggest car I've ever seen purrs along the drive. It's a kind of soft beige colour with darkened windows and a big badge on the bonnet. I assume it must be someone who's got lost.

The car pulls up in front of the house, the driver's door opens and a man steps out. He's wearing a light grey suit and a peaked cap. He walks around to the passenger door and opens it for another chap to get out. I don't know why the second chap is incapable of opening his own door. Perhaps he's disabled. Anyway, he manages to climb out, stands and looks around for a moment, then he walks over towards the front entrance. I wonder if I should offer to help him up the steps but he seems to be managing all right.

"Good evening."

He has a very dark skin but I don't think that's because he's coloured. He looks as though he's been on holiday to Greece for about six years.

"Do you work here?" he asks me.

There's something about the way he speaks that makes me wonder whether he's expecting me to curtsey. I just nod my head instead.

He holds out a hand for me to shake. He's wearing a bright yellow watch. I notice that across the top it has a little window that says, TUESDAY. I've never been able to understand why anyone should need a special gadget for telling them what day of the week it is.

"I'm here to meet my son," he explains. "His name is Wilkinson - Kent Wilkinson. I wonder if you'd be kind enough to let him know I've arrived?"

So this is the famous Old Man Wilkinson. He looks quite young to me.

I hesitate. I feel very tempted to say no. This isn't a hotel and, although I do a lot of dirty jobs, I'm not a servant. I'm certain that Penny would just tell Mr Wilkinson the way to Kent's room and I wonder if I ought to do the same. I don't, though. I set off towards the stairs.

I wouldn't have needed to give him instructions anyway, because you can find Kent's room by following the sound of Iron Maiden erupting along the corridor.

I bang loudly on Kent's door, but of course there's no answer. I try again. I feel like an earwig coughing in an avalanche. In the end, I open the door and walk inside.

It must be less than forty eight hours since I emptied all the rubbish bins and cleaned round the sinks and Alli followed me, dusting and hoovering the carpets. Now this room looks like the aftermath of a jumble sale.

Kent is standing in front of the mirror wearing nothing but a pair of psychedelic boxer shorts, a piece of white cardboard across his chest and a black tie which Arnold is trying to tie for him in a bow. "Your father's here," I tell him.

His face collapses like a watery blancmange.

I'm just backing out of the door as Kent tries to step into his trousers whilst Arnold is still struggling with his tie. "Did you notice if he had a jetski under his arm?" he asks me.

I shake my head, although I wouldn't actually know what a jetski was if I saw one.

"He'll probably have left it in the car," Arnold reassures him.

"Mmmm. Certainly hope so."

I'm edging out of the door because I don't want to stand here gazing at Kent in his underwear, but then he calls me back.

"Jenny, which car is it?" he asks me.

How should I know? I can't tell one car from another. "I don't know."

"There won't be room for it in the Porsche, will there?" says Arnold.

"No, he'd have to bring the Merc. "Look, Jenny..."

I'm back in the corridor now. I don't go back inside; I just stand at the opening of the door. "Mmm?"

"What colour is the car?" He's started speaking really slowly to me. He must think I'm incredibly stupid if I can't tell one car from another. "Is it a brown car or a red one?"

"A light brown colour."

"Right, we're in with a chance then," Kent declares.

Personally, I doubt it very much.

When I've washed the lambs' feeding bottles, I have a quick walk round the grounds before suppertime. I stand and gaze at the fish jumping out of the river, then find I've been standing so long that the sheep creep up

110

behind and start nuzzling me. They make me jump. This has happened to me before. If you stand still for long enough, the sheep nearly always wander over to investigate. They're curious like that.

I set off walking back slowly along the side of the river.

In the rushes there's a reed warbler. I always hear it as I pass. It's an ordinary-looking brown bird which, at one time, I would have thought was a sparrow, but now I know that sparrows don't live in reeds.

Reed warbler is usually confined to reed beds and their borders, I've learned from my bird book.

In the same way, of course, I would once have thought that jackdaws were the same as any other black bird.

It's almost dark now and it's getting cooler.

I climb over the stile and then walk along the path, returning to the front of the house.

I glance up at the clock tower to see if the jackdaws have gone to bed and, suddenly, I see a shape. There's someone standing in the tower, staring down at me.

I feel the blood drain from my face. There can't be anyone in the tower because there isn't any way of getting up there. The tower is derelict. The ladders have all gone rotten. No one's been up there for years.

I stare hard at the tower. There's no mistake about it. I can't tell from this distance whether it's a man or a woman; I just know there's someone there. The figure isn't completely still; it keeps moving slightly. It doesn't seem like the old woman this time. I don't know what it seems like.

The best thing is to tell someone. I can't go around being haunted all the time. I've got to show someone else or I'll start thinking that I'm going mad. I grab all my strength together and run up the steps into the house.

111

"What's the matter, Jenny? Are you all right?"

I almost collide into Bernard, standing by the cheese and biscuits.

I open my mouth to tell him, but all that comes out is a squeak.

"What's the matter? Has something happened?"

I struggle again to tell him, but I don't know what has happened. My voice has disappeared and my shoulders are starting to shake.

He puts his arm round me. "Are you all right?"

I shake my head. I pull Bernard's arm and he follows me out of the door. I cling on to him as we go down the steps. When the tower comes into view, I stare up at it and point. With my other hand, I still hold tightly to Bernard's jacket. "There's someone up there," I manage to whisper hoarsely.

"Whereabouts, Jenny? What do you mean?"

Bernard shakes his head and looks at me as if I'm totally round the twist. Because now, of course, when we look up at the tower, it's completely empty. All we can see is the outline of a jackdaw, standing on the roof.

Sixteen

The following morning, I'm hit on the head by a flying Bertie Bassett.

If it had been at any other time, I don't think I would have minded. You see, it's only a kind of soft toy, like a little man made out of liquorice all sorts.

Bertie is a sort of mascot that Warton has been carrying around, but Kent and Arnold keep grabbing it and using it as a rugby ball or for an impromptu game of cricket along the corridor.

"I say, chaps, has anyone seen Bertie Bassett?" I hear Warton asking in the upstairs corridor.

"Hey, Arnold, catch!"

The next thing I know is that Bertie comes flying downstairs, hits me on the top of the head and then falls into the tureen of left-over porridge on my tray.

"Oh, sos, Jen old girl. Are you all right?"

Of course, it doesn't hurt me because Bertie's only a soft toy.

I try not to show that I'm upset when Kent comes down and takes Bertie, dripping, out of the tureen. "It's okay, Warton. We'll give him the kiss of life," he shouts upstairs. "Just wipe the porridge off his paws, give him a quick heart massage and he'll be smart as a sausage."

I walk down into the kitchen and set the water running for the washing up, but then I stand outside the door and take a few deep breaths. I don't know what's wrong with me. I feel a bit shaky. I feel as though, if somebody crept up behind me and made me jump, I might suddenly burst into tears. That's how I am, as if I could start to cry

113

at any minute

I go back to the kitchen and begin to wash the breakfast things.

I started to feel like this last night after I'd seen the ghost. I felt sort of shaky and upset. Anyway, I don't really think "ghost" is the right name for it, because I suspect that the figure in the clock tower was one of the Belmount boys messing about. Or maybe more than one. I think they got there across the roof.

I decided that because, before I went to bed, I used the bathroom where you can see across the roof to the clock tower. The window was open. People don't normally open it when they're in the bath because there's an extractor fan. I open it when I'm cleaning the bathrooms, but the rest of the time it's shut. There was a half-smoked cigarette by the side of the bath as well. I think they might have climbed out of the window and crawled across the roofs. It would be a really stupid thing to do, but that's how thoughtless they are. They could have been daring each other.

But I don't know what to think about the other ghosts. The old woman and the old-fashioned girl in my bedroom. I haven't seen them again. I think I've been working so hard and getting so much fresh air and wonderful food that, when I go to bed, I always fall asleep straightaway. It was just before I went to sleep when I saw the ghost before. That's if she was a ghost. I don't know.

My room looks different now as well. I've brought my cheese plant from home and my poster with a muddy hippopotamus saying: *A Clean Home is a Sign of a Sick Mind* and my Birds of Britain poster. I've put a calendar up with my days off marked with purple hilighter and, where other teenagers might have photographs of pop

114

stars on their walls, I've got pictures of pigs and sheep and kittens. So it looks like my room. It looks more personal. Maybe the ghost feels out of place.

"So what's the latest on the jetski front then Kent?"

I'm in the upstairs dining room and the boys are at the bottom of the dumb waiter. I can hear them as I'm working. The hatch doors downstairs aren't in the kitchen. They're in the corridor in between the kitchen and the downstairs dining room, the place where the boys queue when they're waiting for the supper bell. I've opened the doors to the hatch at the top and I'm taking out the plates and cutlery.

"Not a single jetski in sight, old chap."

"Your old man not impressed then?"

"That, dear chap, is the understatement of the year."

I set the knives and forks on the big table and then I put out the plates. Then I take out the bowls of horse radish sauce and the fresh bread rolls. I put the pepper and salt out on the table.

"I thought you said he'd got you a presie, though."

Although I'm upstairs in the dining room, I can still hear the long, drawn-out sigh from Kent.

"You couldn't imagine anything more useless."

"What's he bought you? A set of leather-bound maths books?

"The Complete Works of William Shakespeare?"

I send the trolley back down so that Penny can send me the first course. It's roast beef and Yorkshire pud today.

"Well, the first thing I didn't want is extra tuition in Maths...."

Assorted groans emerge from the dumb waiter.

"If that's his idea of an exciting birthday present,"

says Warton, "I'd hate to see his suggestions for hard work."

"The second thing I didn't want is some kind of a family heirloom. It's an old-fashioned watch that they have been saving for my sixteenth birthday."

"Well, perhaps you could sell it."

"Sell it! They'd go spare. I've got to put it in the bank next week."

"Oh."

I hold on to the rope of the trolley. When Penny gives it a little tug. I have to pull it up.

"Have you seen Bertie Bassett? He was here a few minutes ago."

"I don't know where he is. You seen Bertie Bassett, Arnold?"

I hear the hatch doors opening and closing so I start to wind up the trolley. I have to hurry because it's nearly time for the supper bell to ring. The food is supposed to be out on the tables before the grown ups come in.

"Have you got him, Kent?"

"Me? What would I want him for?"

I haul up the trolley to the top and there, sitting on the shelf, grinning at me like an idiot, is Warton's Bertie Basset. There's not a plate of roast beef nor a Yorkshire Pudding in sight.

I feel really cross. I just wish they could understand that some of us have work to do. It's all right for them, playing about. I could get the sack if I don't get my work done on time.

The dinner bell rings in the hall.

I start to get into a panic because all I've done is put out the plates and the bread rolls and horse radish sauce. People will be having to eat horse radish sandwiches whilst they're waiting if the roast beef doesn't come.

116

I send Bertie Bassett crashing back down again and put my head inside the dumb waiter. "Look. Bog off!" I shout down. "And stop getting in my way! Why don't you do something useful for a change?"

"Is everything all right Jenny?"

The voice that comes back isn't that of Kent or any of his friends because, now the bell's gone, they've all gone in to dinner. The only person there is Penny.

"Is this your doll, Jenny? I don't know what you've sent it down here for. Anyway, the roast beef and Yorkshire puddings are on their way up."

Seventeen

Castle Head Field Studies Centre
Grange over Sands
Cumbria
Thursday

Dear Mum
This is just a short note because I don't think I'll have time to write a proper letter for the next few days. The lager louts are here again - the ones I told you about, so everything is very hectic this week. I've survived intact so far, but whether I'll last out the week or not is another matter.

I've just been thinking - after you said you couldn't remember anything more about my mother - whether you could tell me the name of the adoption agency. I thought that perhaps if I wrote to them, they could give me some more information. I thought they might keep the addresses of children's parents, in case they ever wanted to get in touch. It won't do any harm to write to them and find out.

I wanted to say thank you again for putting up with me the other week. And I don't think I said how nice it was to meet Rodney. You seem to be very well suited.

That's all for now.
Lots of love

Jenny

There are leaves and bits of branches scattered across the hall and I've already swept up once this afternoon.

I clamber downstairs to the cleaning cupboard and fetch a sweeping brush and shovel and start all over again. I'm feeling worn out. When the Belmount boys stay here it's like accommodating three primary schools, a safari park and a travelling circus. All at once.

"All for one and one for all!"

I've just about got straight when Kent and Warton come leaping through the doorway into the hall, fencing each other with great long branches.

"On guard!"

"Touché!"

Now I know where all the leaves have come from. "Do you mind?" I ask them. "I'm trying to clean up in here."

"Sos, Jen old girl. Just routing the infidel."

"Well, will you do it somewhere else then, please?"

"Certainly."

They start fencing their way up the staircase.

I sigh deeply.

Just then, Arnold appears in his skin-tight, pink and purple climbing shorts, wearing a laurel wreath on his head. "Hail Caesar!" he calls out, sticking his hand, palm outwards, into the air.

"Hail Brutus!" Kent shouts from the staircase, twisting his leaves into an improvised wreath of victory.

"Salute!"

I pick up as many leaves as I can on my shovel then carry them down to the dustbin.

After that, I decide to take a rest. I'm supposed to have two hours of free time before supper and I've already used up half of it.

First of all, I walk into the dining room and light the

fire. Then the room can be warmed up before supper time. After that, I sit down by the fireside with my magazine. I like to relax in the dining room in the afternoons because it's nice and quiet and I know I won't be disturbed. I pick up my magazine and start thumbing through to find the problem pages. I usually start with those.

I'm just about to stretch out and put my feet up when I hear footsteps outside on the verandah. I look up over the top of Seventeen and I nearly have a heart attack.

It's her, the old woman. The floating-head ghost from the graveyard and the owner of the disembodied voice. I'd recognize her anywhere. She's peering in at me through one of the big windows. I nearly collapse with shock. I stare hard at her face, framed in one of the panes of glass. It looks like a poster for a horror film: there's the huge high window with its golden carved pelmet, the big long curtains, the panes of glass. Then her. She looks like a witch. I give a little involuntary shriek, then dash outside, straight down the hallway and into the library.

I lean back against the shelves of the library, clutching Seventeen against my thudding heart. I feel the blood drain from my face as if I'm going to faint. I don't know what to do.

I look around at the familiar room - the log fire, the coffee tables, the magazines and books. I try to get myself together. I know I mustn't go to pieces. I have to concentrate on the normal things: the light shades, the curtains, the window...

There she is. Again. Staring in at me. Her wrinkled face and her grey hair straggling to her shoulders.

My body seems to lose all substance. I feel in danger of collapsing like a wizzened-up balloon.

The rest of the room is normal. There are shelves of books and piles of magazines. There's someone's dirty coffee mug on the table. There's the stack of logs beside the marble fireplace, and there, peering through the window, standing outside on the verandah, is the old woman.

Her eyes are staring, glaring right at me. She has very deep eye sockets, like a skeleton. For half a second, I find myself staring back at her and then I turn and run. I run out into the hallway.

"Penny!" I'm shouting. "Penny!"

I don't know why I'm shouting for Penny because I haven't seen her all afternoon.

"Penny!" My voice sounds alien. It sounds more like a shriek of terror than a voice.

I feel in a state of total panic because I don't know where to go. I daren't go back in the dining room. I can't go in the library. The verandah goes right around the house so she could be appearing anywhere. I don't know what to do. "Penny!"

I hold on to the edge of the table outside the library, the one where we put the cheese and biscuits. I stand there, motionless, wanting to be sensible. Wanting to be rational, wanting to behave in an adult reasonable manner and all the time, all I want to do is collapse and blackout so that when I come round it will all be over. "Penny!" I shout again.

I'm about to cross the hallway and run downstairs into the kitchen when I freeze. The old woman's standing outside the door with her hand on the door knob, rattling. She's trying to get in.

I flatten myself back against the wall, trying to disintegrate. I don't want her to see me. All I want to do is melt into the wall.

She rattles again on the door knob. She's trying to come inside. I don't know what to do. The door is shaking and I can see her mouth moving, making grotesque shapes.

"Jenny! I think there's someone at the door."

I stare at her as if she's an exhibit in the Chamber of Horrors. She's seen me and she's tapping on the glass, mouthing words at me.

"Aren't you going to answer it?"

Bernard strides through the hallway. He pauses for a second, puzzled, when he sees me, open-mouthed in terror, clinging on to the cheese-dish for support. "Are you all right?" he asks me.

I can't say anything. I just stare, speechless, as he goes to open the door to let the ghost in.

"I'm sorry to keep you waiting," he tells her. "There was no one to answer the door. Can I help you?"

The old woman babbles something incoherent.

"I'm sorry?"

She prattles on again. I think she must be drunk. A drunken ghost. I've never even heard of such a thing.

"Would you like to come inside?"

"The brods," she cackles. "Cedric's brods!"

"Mmm, well, I, er..."

"They've moved the brods. I saw them take the brods!"

"Er, perhaps you'd like to come inside the office. We'll see what we can do."

The old woman stumps in through the door. She's wearing a floor-length, ragged raincoat tied with string. Round her neck she has a kind of woven shawl, all jazzy colours, like purple and gold in a pattern of interlocked circles. She has silver gypsy earrings and on her feet she's got laced-up ankle boots, the kind that very old

122

women sometimes wear in winter, but now of course it's May. They're fastened up with bits of string as well. Across her shoulder is slung a sack with a piece of wood sticking out the top. It looks rather like a skateboard but, because of the way her shoulder is pulled down with the weight, I think it must be heavier than that. It looks as though it's made of iron.

"Are you sure you're okay, Jenny?"

I don't say anything.

"Penny's gone out, by the way. Was it you that was shouting for her?"

I just gaze open-mouthed at Bernard as he strolls across the hallway with the drunken, geriatric gypsy ghost clutching her iron skateboard and leads her inside his office.

Eighteen

"Hello, hello. Is that the, er...whatsitsname?"

Humphrey lounges on the edge of the bed, stark naked except for his smoking jacket and a pair of Japanese sandals. He has just climbed out of a hot bath. Sadly, even a bubble bath and a whole sachet of fresh pine moisture replacement therapy hasn't helped to calm his nerves. The Shifting Sands is turning into a disaster.

"Is that the, er...Theatrecraft? Yes, that's right."

Humphrey pours himself a glass of brandy. "Now, this is Humphrey Head, here. Cumbrian TV. I wonder if you could, er...I'm looking for a model. A female, er...I want to make use of a lady..."

He takes a slurp of brandy then puts his feet up on the bed.

"No, no, not that kind of a model. You've got it all wrong. I want a sort of, er... we've got this lady who isn't too happy about being buried in the sands. That's right, yes, yes. The quicksands. So, I er...was wondering if you could er...do the business."

Humphrey takes off his sandals and tries again to remember how to relax his toes.

"I was wanting a model. That's right, yes. You see, we'll take Lin Dale in close-up when she's, you know, doing the stuff, explaining it all to the viewers, then for the long shots we'll just use a model. We can sink it right down in the sands then winch it out later on with the old whirlybird."

Humphrey winces as he remembers yesterday's horrors with the helicopter. His fingers scour search-

124

ingly across his naked scalp.

"Well, it doesn't really matter who it's a model of you see, darling, because we'll only be seeing it in long shot." He begins to talk much more slowly now, aware that he's conversing with someone who doesn't understand all the technicalities of television. "What've you got in at the moment?"

He starts off with the little toe of his left foot, pressing it into the mattress, then trying to slowly ease off the pressure and relax. "Bertie Bassett? Who's she?"

Humphrey scratches his head. "Mmm, well, super, darling, but I er...I think it really would have to be a female. And I'm not too sure about the liquorice all sorts. Who else have you got?"

"Mrs Tiggiwinkle? Jemima Puddleduck? Well, I don't know if they would, er..."

He shakes his head in confusion. "Margaret Thatcher? No, I don't think..."

Humphrey takes another drink of brandy. "Look, just let us have whatever you think is suitable. If you can deliver it down to Grange over Sands tomorrow morning. And, er, there's just one other thing..."

He presses even harder on his left toe in a vain attempt to float it away inside the mattress of his hotel bed. "Do you have a selection of blond hairpieces? Something sort of young and virile. Super. Well, if you could send a couple of those down as well, everything'll be hunky-dory."

"Are we going to get a look at this watch then, Kent?"

"I'll bring it down," says Kent. "Just a tick."

After the word "tick" he poses on the staircase in his salopettes with his arms extended waiting for the appreciation for his joke.

Everyone just groans.

I'm sitting on a hard-backed chair in the corridor with a cup of tea. I still feel in a state of shock.

Kent disappears upstairs to his bedroom whilst the others gather round enthusing about his watch. "He's going to have to keep it in the bank, you know. It'll be too much of a temptation."

"That's right. He'll be taking it down the old pawn-brokers."

"His old man says it's worth a few grand."

I'm trying to sort out in my mind about the old woman. You see, the person/thing/being that has just walked with Bernard into his office didn't look like a ghost. It looked very much like a scruffy old gypsy in an ancient raincoat tied with string. I just don't know what to think.

"He'll be trying to pawn it next week."

"Buying a jetski with the money."

And yet I feel sure that she's been following me. Or haunting me. She didn't seem like a normal person when her eyes were peering at me through the window of the church; and the humming in the garden - that didn't sound like the voice of a normal person either. And I feel sure that both of them were her.

"Here you are then, chaps!"

"Da da daaaa!"

Kent descends the staircase with his own improvised fanfare of trumpets. He thinks so much of himself, that boy. I find myself almost wanting him to trip up. I don't think I've ever felt like that about anyone before. I find it very disturbing. I see a little picture of him in my mind, tripping over and tumbling headlong down the staircase and I can't help having a little smile. I know it's wicked to think about people like that but I just can't help myself.

"Here we are then. One family heirloom in solid gold. Gentleman's pocket watch circa 1780."

Kent takes the watch out of its box and dangles it by a long golden chain. I glance up at it. The face has parts that are sparkling; I think it must be inlaid with jewels. There's a design as well, painted on the front. In spite of myself, I stand up, fascinated, and walk across to try and get a closer look.

"Oh, wizzo!"

"Not bad, eh?"

"Bit more style than the old Rolex, eh?"

Kent doesn't speak to me, but he holds the watch out to show me when I walk across. On the face it has a painting of an iron bridge. The bridge spans a wooded valley and, in the river at the bottom, you can see the reflection of the bridge, forming a complete circle. What is so amazing is the detail. The brushwork is so delicate; it must have been done with the tiniest paintbrush. I've never seen anything like it.

"Good bit of workmanship there."

"Reckon it must be worth a bit."

Kent turns it over. "Got the family crest here on the back."

And there is the picture of the entwined serpents, only this time it's engraved in gold, beautifully-wrought with fancy scrolls. I can see the eyes of the serpents and their tails and tiny scales.

There's a disturbance behind me and the old woman appears, gawping across my shoulder.

"What is that?"

Kent starts to put the watch back in its box.

"Let me see."

Her voice is nasty and vicious. I look around and I'm

127

amazed to see her eyes. She doesn't look like the same person. Whereas her eyes were pale and grey before, now they're red and blazing. Her voice is loud and strident. It doesn't sound like the voice of an old woman or a ghost; it sounds too powerful and strong.

"Show me!"

Everyone cowers away. They seem afraid of her. Even Kent, who towers above her in size, starts to draw back.

"Show me," she demands.

Reluctantly, Kent removes the watch again and holds it out for her to see.

"I told you." She wags her finger at him. "I told you it was an evil sign."

Kent looks puzzled. He looks frightened as well. All his confidence has gone.

"You should have thrown back the clasp where you found it..."

Kent shakes his head from side to side.

"You should have thrown it straight back in the sands."

When he makes no answer, she speaks to all of us. She reminds me of a character I saw once in a stage play. "Back in the shifting sands," she calls out. "Back in the shifting sands!" She sounds like some kind of ancient prophetess or...I remember it now.... one of the witches in Macbeth.

Then she points a crooked finger at Kent. "Throw that evil charm straight back into the sands," she tells him.

Kent still can't think what to say.

Bernard comes to his rescue. "Can I show you out?" he asks the old woman politely, taking her by the arm.

"Back in the shifting sands!" she shouts as he leads her away down the hall.

"Well, I hope you can find your way back all right."

"I told him that it was an evil charm. The sign of the Celtic Dead."

"Yes, I'm sure you did."

"Buried three times, I told him."

"Mmm."

"Three times."

"If you follow the drive, it'll lead you straight down to the gate."

"You make sure he does it," she shouts as she hobbles down the front steps. "Throw it straight back in the shifting sands!"

Nineteen

I go upstairs to get washed and changed before supper.

I still feel taken aback. I feel a bit weak and shaky. There are so many things I have to think about and sort out and I don't know where to start.

I feel worried about the strange woman. I hope she doesn't come back here any more. I don't want her haunting me again. The other thing is that I realize how, in the last few days, I've done several things wrong. I've been trying really hard to do my work properly and make a good impression, but since the Belmount boys returned, nearly everything has gone to maggots.

I hope I don't get the sack. I start to itemize my main moments of failure as I wait for the hot water to run into the sink.

Firstly, I told Bernard there was someone in the clock tower when there wasn't and he saw me collapsing in the courtyard like a lolly without its stick. I cringe when I think how embarrassed I felt, pointing up at the clock tower when there was nothing there more frightening than a jackdaw.

Secondly, I swore at Penny down the hatch. I feel a shiver when I remember hearing her voice soaring up through the dumb waiter. It was bad enough, sending her a Bertie Basset crashing down on the trolley, but swearing made it worse. It didn't help either when I apologized and tried to explain by telling her that I thought she was Kent and Arnold. "But we're not supposed to swear at the customers, either, Jenny," she told me.

I didn't know what to say.

I put the plug in the sink when the hot water comes through and then I start to wash my face.

Then, this afternoon, when I should have been opening the front door to let the two hundred-year-old gypsy inside, Bernard came across me, as white as a snowman in a stupor.

I remember what he said at my interview: We'll employ you on a temporary basis for the first few months. That'll give us a chance to get to know each other. See whether you think this is the kind of environment you want to work in or not. And see whether we think you're suitable.

I've got a horrible feeling that they won't find me suitable at all.

I finish getting changed just as I hear the bell downstairs for dinner. I leave my room and walk along the corridor. We're all eating in the lower dining hall today because the only other adults here are Marjorie and Dr Lune.

As I'm walking down the corridor, I hear music blaring out. I don't know if music is the right word; it's the Gothic, heavy-metal stuff coming from Kent's bedroom. Presumably, the music is so loud that he hasn't heard the supper bell. I knock on his door to let him know.

There's no answer. I don't want to barge in and find him in his underwear again. I knock once more.

The door is open slightly, so I just push it a little bit. If he's gone downstairs already, I'll turn his cassette player off. I don't see why we should have it disturbing everyone in the house.

I look inside and the room is empty. I can see the ghetto-blaster on his desk over by the window so I walk across and press the PAUSE button. There's instant silence. That's better. By the side of the recorder is an empty cassette box - The Celtic Dead - it says across the top with a picture of some blokes with long hair, leather jackets and hippy headbands. All I can say is that they make a lot of noise for Dead Celts. Or, as Warton would put it, if they're the Dead Celts, I'd hate to hear what the live ones sound like.

On the table is the velvet box, standing half open with the watch inside. I'd like to pick up the watch and look at it more closely, but I know I mustn't. I just open the lid a bit more and take a little peep. I look at the picture on the front. I notice the detail in the background - trees on the side of the hills and branches on the trees. I can even see a little bird, painted on one of the branches.

As I'm about to turn away, I notice that, at the bottom of the watch there are some initials, so tiny you can hardly read them: J.W. Mmm. Those aren't Kent's initials; he's K.W. But then it wasn't his watch until last night. He said it was a family heirloom.

And, on the back, he said it had the family crest. The ring of serpents. Although I know I shouldn't, I just take the watch out of its box for a moment and turn it over. There they are, carved in gold and snarling. I look at their tiny eyes and their golden scales. It's the crest that was carved on the tree outside with the same initials, of course: J.W.

Things are falling into place now, but why should the crest seem so familiar? Why do I always feel as though I've seen it somewhere before? It isn't my family crest; it's his. But that's just what it feels like - as if it belongs to me and my family; I feel as though the crest is something to do with me and my history, rather than with someone else.

I know I shouldn't be holding the watch. It's a good job I've just got washed or I'd have put grubby finger marks all over it. I pack it back carefully inside the velvet box and close the lid. No one will know, of course, and I haven't done any harm.

I think I'd better go down to supper.

I'm just walking out into the corridor, closing the door behind me, when Warton appears. When he sees me, he pauses for a moment. I suppose he's wondering what I've been doing in Kent's room. "I've just been in to turn Kent's tape recorder off," I explain. "It was driving me round the bend."

Warton doesn't say anything; he just sprints downstairs to the dining room.

I walk in to supper. I never feel very relaxed, eating my meals down here because it always seems so noisy. It's a bit like school - thirty people all eating together in one big room. I walk across and sit in the empty place next to Bernard.

"Would you like some roast pork?" he asks me. "And some apple sauce?"

"Thank you." I start to fill up my plate.

"I've just got to make an announcement." Bernard stands up and bangs his spoon on the table. "Can you listen for a minute, please?"

He waits until everyone is quiet before he carries on. "A local person," he explains, "a certain lady, came to see me this afternoon."

I help myself to roast potatoes.

"She was very concerned about the branches which some of you had brought back from the beach."

Not the mad woman. The geriatric ghost.

"Now I think I've mentioned to you before that these sprigs of laurel - or brods, as they call them locally -

have a very important function."

I wonder whether to have French beans or carrots and decide that perhaps I could manage a bit of both.

"The local guide, Cedric Robinson, cuts branches of laurel to mark the pathway across the sands. He plants these brods in the sand at low tide. And he would still expect to find them there, several tides later, to assist him when he's taking a party of people across the bay."

I remember now. That's why Cedric has this massive laurel hedge outside his cottage.

"I assume that you'd forgotten what I'd told you about this..." Bernard deliberately stresses the word, "assume" as though he really suspects they might have collected up the brods on purpose, "when you were stupid enough to pull up the branches and bring them back." He looks round at the groups of boys, some of whom lower their eyes and look a bit shame-faced.

Bernard, of course, used to be a schoolteacher. That's why he's so good at telling people off. I think Dr Lune and Marjorie could pick up some lessons from him; they're the ones who are supposed to be in charge of looking after this load of hooligans.

"I shouldn't need to explain that, in moving the brods, you could have been responsible for people getting into great difficulties on the sands and perhaps even losing their lives. I have told you before that the sands here are extremely dangerous, but I think perhaps I need to mention that again. There are hidden channels of water, there are quicksands and the tide can come in suddenly and cut you off. Just remember that no one must go across the sands without the help of the local guide, Cedric Robinson."

Bernard gives a little nod to show that the lecture's over and then he sits down. I'm very pleased because I was getting worried about my dinner going cold.

"Would you like some boiled potatoes as well, Jenny?" he asks me.

"Well, I'll perhaps just manage one or two."

The roast pork is scrummy, just like all the meals at Castle Head. The vegetables always taste good as well.

When we've finished, I pick up our plates and take them over to Alli who's taking her turn at serving behind the hatch. "That was very nice, thank you," I tell her.

"I'll let the chef know you enjoyed it," she grins. I happen to know that it's Alli herself who's the chef today.

I scrape off the left-over food then place the cutlery into the bowl of hot soapy water.

"We'll have to watch out for old Gertie Gasbag then, next time we're out," I hear someone say behind me.

"Dirty Gertie!"

"Dirty Gertie on her skateboard!"

"The brods! The brods!" Someone starts to imitate the old woman's voice. "Who's been pulling up Cedric's brods?"

"If she's a lady," says Warton, "I'd hate to think what the old tramps look like round here."

I pick up a big bowl of apple crumble and some custard for our table.

Just as I'm turning round, I hear Kent and Arnold behind me. "Is it still on then, for tomorrow?" I hear Arnold ask.

"I don't see why not."

"Well, I just thought, you know, with what he was saying..."

I look up at Kent, wondering what they're planning now.

135

He shrugs his shoulders. "Sounds to me like a big fuss about nothing."

I don't know what he means by that. I don't think I want to either. I go back to my place next to Bernard and dish out the apple crumble.

"Thank you, Jenny," says Bernard, as he pours himself an extra-large helping of custard. "Listen, I was wondering if you wouldn't mind giving me a hand later on."

"What do you want me to do?"

I share out the rest of the crumble then sit down and start to eat.

"Well, I'm giving a talk after supper. I wondered if you'd mind helping out with the slides."

"No, I'd be glad to," I tell him, "but I've never done it before. I wouldn't really know what to do."

"Well, I'll have the slides all in order," he explains, "and you can work the projector. I'll just give you a nod when I'm ready to move on."

I've never worked a slide projector but perhaps I'll be able to pick it up as I go along. "What's the talk about?" I ask him.

"It's just another of my talks about the history of Castle Head and the Wilkinson family, but this time it's with illustrations."

"All right." I smile at him and try to look intelligent.

Twenty

"Now here are the slides," Bernard explains. "They're all in order starting from the front."

That seems easy enough. It just means I have to take them out one at a time and work backwards.

"Each slide has a yellow dot on the top so you know which way up to put them. You see, you always put them upside down and back to front."

I nod my head and try to look competent.

"So you take out a slide and place it here, like this, move it along like this..." Bernard gives me a demonstration. "Then whilst that slide's showing, you can get the next one ready, put it in here...move it along like so...then you take that one out and put the next one in. Do you see what I mean?"

"Mmm, I think so."

"When you've taken them out, I should put them all in a pile over here, then you won't get them mixed up. If you could keep them in the same order, it would be helpful. Is that all right?"

I could really do with a bit of a practice before we start, but I don't like to suggest it. I don't want him to think I'm totally useless.

"If any of them seem a bit out of focus, you can twirl this little knob here, but I think you'll find that it's adjusted all right."

The projector is lit up and shining on to a large white screen next to Bernard's table where his books and notes have been set out beside a large mug of steaming coffee.

Suddenly, the door flies open and there's a mass invasion.

"Saturday night at the movies!"

"Where are we sitting, chaps?"

"Where's the lady with the ice cream and the popcorn?"

"Saturday night at the movies!"

The Belmount boys don't sit properly on the chairs. Instead, they lounge about with their feet up on the seats, prodding and poking each other and shouting and singing stupid songs. Then they start making shadow puppets on the screen. The primary school children we had staying here behaved as if they were a lot more grown up. Someone makes a rabbit with long pointed ears, then starts singing the Bugs Bunny tune. "What's up, doc?" he croaks.

Then somebody else makes a crocodile that creeps along like a large pair of scissors and snips off the rabbit's ears. They seem to think this is all very funny.

I place the first slide in the shutter, ready for when Bernard begins his talk.

"Right then," he starts off, "when you're all ready." He waits for everyone to settle down. "An illustrated history of Castle Head."

He gives me a nod to indicate that it's time for the first slide and I wham in the picture of Castle Head, with all the buildings upside down. The house is balancing on the clock tower with a slightly distressed-looking jackdaw underneath.

There are hoots of derision from the Belmount boys. "Poor old bird, eh? Having to hold all this place up."

"Must be giving him a headache."

"I'm sorry," I start to mutter.

"It's okay, Jen old girl. We'll all stand on our heads if

138

it makes it any easier."

"Now, that of course is the building with which you're all familiar..." says Bernard.

"Never seen it before in our lives, have we chaps?" I hear Arnold mutter.

"Never. We'd have remembered it."

"Defies all the laws of gravity."

"If that's supposed to be familiar, I'd hate to see something strange."

"And here," Bernard goes on, "is our very productive farm."

Yellow is the top and the slide is supposed to be upside down so I put it in yellow-side downwards and get a picture of a flotilla of sheep all lying flat on their backs with their legs sticking straight up in the air.

This causes even more hilarity. "Sheep don't look too healthy, eh what?"

"Look about ready for the old mutton cutlets to me."

"If that's the productive farm, I'd hate to see the one that's losing business."

Yellow, I decide, really is on the top because the slides have already been turned upside down.

I get it organized at last and off we go with the story of John Wilkinson, the ironmaster who worked with James Watt making steam engines and who built the house at Castle Head.

Yellow on the top and I remember not to put my thumb in front of the picture. I push the slide forwards then take the old one out and put a different one in. I place the ones we've seen over on my right and try to keep them all in order.

"In the last twenty years of his life, Wilkinson seemed troubled by the fact that he had no son to succeed him."

I wham in a picture of John Wilkinson, looking

slightly troubled.

"His first wife died whilst giving birth to his daughter; his second wife had no children at all and, later in life, Wilkinson began to patronize his nephew, Thomas Jones, presumably with hopes of bringing him into the family business."

At the words, "family business", Bernard keeps nodding his head and I move on to a sequence of pictures of different kinds of steam engines and iron bridges.

"Yet in the 1790s, when he was almost seventy years old, John Wilkinson took a mistress. He formed a relationship with one of his servants...This girl, Anne Lewis, bore him three children: a daughter Mary Anne, another daughter Joanna and then, in 1806 when Wilkinson was 78 years old, at last she gave birth to the son for whom he'd been waiting all his life."

My hand falters. He took a mistress, Anne Lewis...a servant girl, Lewis...

"Are you ready, Jenny?"

I look up. "Sorry." I push the slide along.

I think of two things, both at once: firstly, my real mother who worked in a hotel; my mother that I've been looking for; her name was Lewis.

"John Wilkinson died soon after his son was born. This house and all his property was left to Anne Lewis and her three children..."

And secondly, the servant...the strange woman in my room. She was talking about a man who it seemed had...

There's a pause.

"I think there are two pictures there at once, Jenny..."

I look up and see that the people on the picture all have two heads.

"Sorry."

140

"She'd need all that money to feed them all," Kent mutters.

"Certainly would," says Arnold, "if they all had two heads."

"Of course, Wilkinson's nephew, Thomas Jones, contested the will. Anne Lewis's children were illegitimate and Thomas claimed that he was the only legally rightful heir."

You see, I'm wondering whether this Anne Lewis could be some distant relative of my mother's, some kind of ancestor. And that would mean that...

"After this there was a long legal battle. The solicitors fought very hard... " There's another pause. "Jenny?"

I've been so busy thinking I've forgotten to get the next slide ready. I pick up the nearest slide and push it through. It's the upside down sheep again.

"Baaaa."

"Baaaaaaa."

"Funny-looking solicitors."

"Don't seem to be fighting too hard either."

"If those were fighting hard, I'd hate to see what the docile ones looked like."

"What's the matter, Jenny?"

"Sorry." I bang in another picture of a steam engine.

Bernard stands there shaking his head. He's starting to look a bit annoyed.

"Sorry. I seem to have got them a bit mixed up."

Bernard takes a long drink of his coffee. It must be nearly cold by now.

"And it was during this time that Castle Head fell into disrepair. The house was left standing empty and the gardens became overgrown."

Bernard raises his eyebrows at me hopefully and I look down at the slides. I can't see a picture that looks anything like an overgrown garden. I find something that I think looks like a tree, but when I put it on it turns out to be a goat.

Everybody cracks out laughing.

"I suppose the family bought the goat to help eat all the overgrown grass," chuckles Arnold.

People start making goat noises and Bernard looks even more annoyed.

"Right, perhaps if you'd like to turn the projector off for a minute, Jenny..." he says.

I know he hasn't really finished all the slides. He just doesn't want me spoiling his talk any more.

"We can let it cool down for a minute."

Bernard finishes off his coffee. "Well," he continues, "we're very fortunate tonight in having an extra special illustration for this talk, something which very few people have ever had the opportunity to see before."

"Now..." he looks a bit brighter when he sees that everyone's looking interested "...obviously, there were people who did inherit some of the Wilkinson fortune and who still have some evidence of that today. We have with us Kent Wilkinson, who most of you know..."

Kent stands up and gives a stupid bow which isn't at all necessary as everyone knows who he is.

"Kent's great great grandfather...I think that's right...?" Bernard looks up for confirmation, but Kent is still grinning inanely at the audience.

"He inherited much of what was left of the Wilkinson fortune and this week, I understand, Kent has received the famous Wilkinson watch...I wonder if you'd be kind enough to fetch it and show us, Kent...?"

Kent nods cheerfully, always happy for an opportunity to show off. He walks past me and out of the door.

When Kent has gone, Bernard carries on. "This watch

has been handed down from father to son in every generation on the date of the son's sixteenth birthday. Kent will be placing the watch in a safe deposit next week, so this is a rare opportunity to actually see it."

I walk across and open the curtains. They won't be able to see the watch very well in the dark.

"And what you'll be able to see painted on the watch is the famous iron bridge - the one I told you about, the one that spans the River Severn..."

I look out across the verandah and the river and the meadows and the trees and it occurs to me suddenly that, if my family really is descended from Anne Lewis, then perhaps all this really should be mine.

Sandy, sitting smartly as always on the front row, asks suddenly, "Is that why Kent's family's so rich then, sir?"

Bernard seems unsure. "Well, Sandy, they inherited their money originally but then I'm sure they've invested it very wisely."

And what if I'd had it? What would I have done with it? I look outside. Perhaps I am the rightful owner of all this. As far as the eye can see: the river and the fields, the farm and the tractor, the sheep and the goats, the house and all its furniture. Even the walled garden, the Celtic hill fort. Perhaps all this really should be mine. Perhaps it should have belonged to my mother and my grandmother and my great grandmother and her mother. Perhaps the ring of serpents should be mine: the family crest. My family crest. Perhaps that's why I know it's so familiar.

The idea is too much for me to contemplate. I look outside again and see a figure walking by the side of the river. I think it's the old woman. I don't feel terrified of her now. Not now I've seen her properly. She's holding her skate board underneath her arm. It has two handles on it.

"Here we are." Bernard looks up expectantly as Kent walks in through the door.

But as soon as I see Kent, I know that something's wrong. He's holding the velvet box in his hand, but his face is as white as bleach. He has a look of distress the way he did when the old woman confronted him in the hall outside. His confidence has disappeared together with his perky grin.

He holds up the box to show Bernard and the box is empty. "I left it out in my room," he tells him. He shakes his head in disbelief. "I left the watch out in my room just before I came downstairs. Just before supper." He looks around at all of us, sitting open-mouthed and staring at him. His face is pale with shock. "The watch is worth thousands of pounds," he tells us. "Someone's been in my room and taken it." He shakes his head with a look of confusion on his face. "They've been in my room and they've stolen the Wilkinson watch."

Twenty one

Drrrr drrrr. Drrrrr drrrrrr.

Drrrr drrrr. Drrrrr drrrrrr.

Humphrey turns over and buries his head in the pillow.

Drrrr drrrr. Drrrrr drrrrrr.

The sound of the phone is like a road drill across his scalp.

Drrrr drrrr. Drrrrr drrrrrr.

He squeezes the pillow across his ears, but still the sound refuses to go away.

Drrrr drrrr. Drrrrr drrrrrr.

Humphrey has a hangover.

His hand fumbles out of the duvet towards the telephone. The ringing stops and he grunts. "Hnnggg."

"Hello. Is that you, Humphrey?"

"Hnngggg."

"Humphrey, it's Cartmel here. We're all waiting for you. Are you all right?"

Humphrey feebly opens one eye to peer at the illuminated digital display by the side of the telephone. Sugar lumps. He should have been there an hour ago.

"Are you still there?"

"Hnnnhhhggg."

"The crew are all set up. We've got the model and everything. They want to get started soon because the weather doesn't look too good."

Humphrey makes a superhuman effort to sit up and encounter reality. Someone seems to have built a motorway underneath his scalp and buses, motorbikes and articulated lorries are booming through his head. "Super, darling," he says. He doesn't know what is super or even, what is so endearing about the woman he is talking to, but there is something reassuring about the sound of his own voice saying things he's heard himself say so many times before. "Absolutely super."

Humphrey's breakfast consists of two Paracetamol and a large glass of brandy which he drinks as he pulls on his thermal underwear. It can get very cold, standing in the middle of the mudflats. He selects a fleecy cotton two-tone, orange and tan shirt to wear with his Paisley plum cravat before putting on his leather jacket. It's a good job, he thinks to himself, that some people still keep up certain standards of appearance. He checks himself in the mirror and winces. His first job will have to be to buy himself a hat.

The local shops are sparse and mainly closed. There's Patterson's News, Lambert's Fruit and Veg, The Golden Dragon Chinese take-away and a petrol station. Nowhere to buy a hat. There's also a howling gale outside. Humphrey is two hours late already, but how can he appear on location with his scalp completely bald? And what's the point of buying a hat that will blow away immediately in the gale?

Humphrey walks into the nearby garage to obtain the advice of a local resident. The owner comes out, unhooks the petrol pump and starts looking round for Humphrey's car. "Do you want 4-star?" he asks. "We haven't got unleaded."

"I was, er....not really, I was looking for an, er...I was looking for a hat."

The garage owner looks disconcerted until he remembers his stock of left-over headgear from last season. "Come in." He invites Humphrey into his office.

They walk into a grease-lined shed filled with jacks and ramps, tyres and spanners, disused Visa slips and Girlie calendars. A small transistor balanced on the shelf crackles out a list of requests:

This one's for Mr and Mrs Arnside and their son, Jason, their daughter, Kylie and Bungo the dog...

Underneath one of the workbenches are a couple of battered old cardboard boxes. "Here you are."

And it's for Norman and Janice in Fleetwood Terrace, Blackpool, the best cat in the world...

The garage owner pulls out a couple of children's baseball hats, a few chef's hats that were given away free with last year's barbecues and a cowboy hat with KISS ME QUICK AND FEEL ME SLOWLY around the brim.

It's for Jan and Stephen on the rock stall at Blackpool Pleasure Beach and for Suki and Jazz..

"You don't have a sort of little black beret with a...."

Then Humphrey spots the elastic underneath the cowboy hat which, hopefully, will attach it to his scalp until he collects his new toupé. "No, no, that will do fine, thank you. Just the business. How much er...how much is it?"

The garage owner removes the 75p sticker deftly from the back. "£6.50"

"Super. Absolutely super."

I'm sorry we don't have the record that you've all requested, but ...something which will more than compensate... the latest number by the country's new sensational rock band appearing in this area tomorrow evening. Yes, you know who I mean, folks - the one and only - Celtic Dead!"

Humphrey tries the hat on. "Yes, darling, I think this looks rather fetching." He removes the KISS ME

147

QUICK label and places it inside his pocket. He doesn't see the FEEL ME SLOWLY sticker at the back. "Yes, I think I'll cause quite a sensation in this."

The garage owner isn't sure what to think.

As I walk upstairs, I see Warton coming out of Bernard's office.

There's no reason to be upset about that; he can come out of Bernard's office if he wants to; but what does upset me is the look on Warton's face, or rather, the look on Warton's face when he sees me.

I wouldn't expect him to be friendly or even particularly civil; I might have expected him to nod or smile or maybe say hello, but he doesn't. That isn't what worries me; it's the fact that he looks away quickly when he sees me. He looks away sheepishly and then stops in his tracks as though he's just realized he's forgotten something, then turns and start to walk the other way. I know that's because he doesn't want to pass me on the stairs. I know why as well.

It turns my stomach over. I remember something similar happening once before. It was when my mum and dad got divorced. I went to court with my mum and, although I kept telling myself that I wasn't worried about it, when the time came to actually go to court, I was very upset. I felt as if we were criminals, as if we'd done something wrong. I kept telling myself that of course they could get divorced if they wanted to and it wasn't anything to do with me. But when we had to sit in the waiting room in the county court with all the other mums and children, I started feeling sick.

I sat staring out of the window, trying to keep a hold of myself and trying not to cry and then the door opened and, for some reason, I looked round, and there was my father, standing in the doorway. I started to smile and

148

began to lift my hand to wave to him. I'm certain that he saw me. But then he turned around and walked outside, just as if I wasn't there. Just as if he hadn't seen me. Just as if I didn't exist any more. He was refusing to acknowledge my existence.

And that's what Warton's doing. Refusing to acknowledge my existence.

I finish my jobs and then the rest of the day is free. Normally, I really enjoy my free time; I walk into the village and buy some postcards and ice cream or I stroll down to the beach or explore the countryside with my bird book. Today, I feel in danger of exploding.

I walk upstairs to my room and the first thing I notice is an envelope with my name on stuck to my door with Blu tak. I take down the envelope and walk into my room and I notice that my hands are shaking.

I think about making myself a cup of tea; I think about having some cheese and biscuits; I think about curling up underneath my eiderdown with a magazine. I think about running away.

If it wasn't important, you see, it wouldn't be inside an envelope. There wouldn't be any need to seal it up. There's a little yellow, self-adhesive message pad in the office for messages. People just fill in the boxes and scribble notes like: Jen, your mum rang - Wed. pm. that sort of thing. They don't put them in sealed envelopes.

I sit down on the edge of the bed. I feel sick as I open the envelope and take out the piece of notepaper.

Dear Jenny,
I would like to see you as there are one or two things we need to have a chat about. Could you call in the office between two and three?
Bernard.

Twenty two

"Hello, darlings!"

"Oh, there you are, Humphrey."

"Just when we're about ready to pack up for lunch," Cartmel mutters under her breath.

"Morning, darling!" Humphrey twirls across to Lin Dale and gives her a brandy-infected slobbery kiss on the cheek. "Learned all our lines, have we?"

Lin, who has known her script word-perfect for the last three weeks, waits until Humphrey has moved away before she wipes her cheek. She exchanges glances with Cartmel who also has to endure the assault of the great slobbery lips.

The camera crew discreetly edge out of the way.

"Right then, let's do the business. Take one. Off we go."

"Mmm, Humphrey..." Cartmel walks across hesitantly with her clipboard. "We were just wondering..."

"Everything hunky-dory, is it darling?"

"The, er...the model..." Cartmel points to the human-sized model of Mrs Tiggiwinkle which the crew have spent most of the morning embedding in the sand.

Humphrey glances in the direction of her immaculately-varnished finger tip. "Sweet sugar! What's that? It looks like a giant hedgehog."

"It's the model you ordered: Mrs Tiggiwinkle."

"It's what? I never asked for a ten foot hedgehog."

"That's what it says on the order sheet, Humphrey: Mrs Tiggiwinkle. We couldn't quite understand why you er...anyway, they sent some blond wigs as well. We've put one on it to try and cover up its prickles."

Humphrey stares in horror at the hedgehog. "What ever does it look like?" he asks the chief cameraman. "Have you tried it out in long shot?"

The cameraman nods. "It looks just like a giant hedgehog," he explains.

I start to pack my case. I open my top drawer and take out my socks and underwear and put those in first and then I start on my jumpers and my jeans. I'm not going to let them sack me. I know they think I've taken Kent Wilkinson's watch; I knew that as soon as I saw Warton walking out of Bernard's office. I knew he'd been to see Bernard to tell him he'd seen me leaving Kent's room the night before. I know they think I'm not suitable for working here as well; I could tell that when I was doing the slides for Bernard and getting them all in a mess. All the time, he was probably watching me and thinking. He was thinking how they could get rid of me and employ somebody more intelligent.

I start to take down my posters. I take off the bits of Blu tak and squash them up into a ball and roll the posters up together. I take down Snoopy's "I Hate Mondays" poster and the picture of the mud-soaked hippopotamus saying "A clean home is the first sign of a sick mind." I take down the Birds of Britain poster and the wall calendar with my days-off marked in purple hilighter and the pictures of the pigs and kittens. And all the time there's this thing welling up inside me like a monkey. It's big and hairy and it claws its way up through my stomach as if it's trying to escape.

I remember when I brought my posters a few weeks ago. When I went home for the weekend and I felt as though everything had changed. I felt as though my mother was starting a life of her own without me. That's

when I brought all my posters back with me on the train
and I thought to myself, "Well, this is my new home
now. This is where I live - in Castle Head. This is my
new family. I'm grown up now and I don't live at home
with my mum any more."

I start to pack my writing paper and my pencil box,
my snowman hot water bottle and my bird book. I don't
know where to put the Blu tak. I lay it in a wedge, down
on the table, and then I walk outside for some fresh air.

I go out the back way so I don't have to go near
Bernard's office. I shan't go to see him this afternoon. I
shan't go to see him at all. I know what he's going to
say. He's going to tell me I'm dismissed. I just want to
go and get out of their way so they can employ
somebody they think is suitable.

I walk up the mound. I walk up the hill behind the
house. I walk through the trees and then I turn off the
path and make my way through the undergrowth until
I'm at the bottom of the old walled garden. And then I
find the special seat, the one that's built into the outside
wall. I sit there on the broken bench where all the bits of
rustic wood are riddled with woodworm and peeling off
the walls, and I realize that's just how I feel; I feel like
something in an old, neglected garden; I feel as though
nobody wants me any more. I feel abandoned.

I try not to give way to self-pity. I've always believed
that, when bad things happen, there's always something
good ahead that you can look forward to. My mum
always used to say that every dark cloud has a silver
lining. I used to believe in that but, at the moment, I
think that she's found the silver lining to her cloud, and
maybe there isn't one for me. Right now I can't think of
anything at all to look forward to. All I can think of is
how much I've enjoyed my work at Castle Head. It

hasn't been easy but I've enjoyed it more than I've ever liked anything before. The only thing I've been dreading is that, if they thought I wasn't suitable, I might have to go back home, back home to the dole.

There are voices behind me, at the back of the wall. They're not spooky voices this time; it isn't the mad woman, humming away; I think it's some of the boys from Castle Head. They must have climbed up the other path and gone round inside the old garden from the other entrance.

"Well, it's our only chance of seeing The Celtic Dead. They won't do another gig up here."

"They might do one later on."

"No chance. And anyway, we'd all be away before long, for the summer."

"I'll be in Florida."

"We'll be in the South of France."

"Well, there you are, you see. I'll be in the Seychelles. I'll be completely and utterly bored. There'll be nothing to do all day but sit on the beach, gazing at the scenery. It'll be painful."

"I mean, I do want to see them. It's just what that chap, Bernard was saying - I just don't feel too happy about us getting back. We don't want to finish up being sucked down into the quicksands."

"No such thing old chap, no such thing."

"What do you mean?"

"Well, it's just an old wives' tale, isn't it? Sands that suck you down into the earth? And where are they likely to suck you down to, eh? Into the centre of the earth and straight through to Australia? Quick look at the Test Match then schluck! straight back home?"

"Well, that chap Bernard seemed to think it was serious."

153

"Oh, that's just scaremongering. It's like - do you remember those lectures we had in the hall last term on the dangers of alcoholism, just because they'd found us with four cans of lager each...?"

"They must think we've got the brain cells of a bunch of earwigs."

"So, you reckon that because they lecture us about walking across the sands, it doesn't really mean they think we might drown."

"No. It's just to make sure they're covered, isn't it?"

"I'll tell you what, I'll have a look in the Tide Tables if you like..."

"What's that?"

"It's a kind of chart that tells you what time the tide comes in. I think old Bernard'll have one in his office."

"Oh, that sounds handy. Do you think he'll let us borrow it?"

"No, but I can just sneak in and have a look. I don't think he bothers to leave the office locked."

"Right then, we'll be all set. Bring your buckets and spades, chaps. And we'll stop off and make some sand castles on the way back home."

Twenty three

It's starting to rain again. I could stay here on the seat, where it's a bit sheltered, but then the boys might see me when they come out; I don't want them to guess that I've been listening to their conversation for the last five minutes.

Anyway, it's beginning to feel cold. There's a strong wind blowing, bowing down the branches of the trees. I don't want to be caught out here in a storm. I stand up. I know I'm going to get wet, but I'll get wetter if I stay. I haven't brought a hat, but I turn up the collar on my mac and then start to run back down the hillside, making sure I don't slip, keeping my head down, watching out for stones and tree roots on the path.

I head towards the back of Castle Head. That's because the back door's nearest and also because I still don't want to go past Bernard's office.

I turn the corner into the yard. It's more exposed here; the wind is blowing and the rain comes lashing down. I lower my head, ready to make a dash for it, when suddenly, I stop dead in my tracks.

There's a police car. A police car is parked in the yard outside the back door of Castle Head. I screech to a halt. Because the police car flashes a warning in my head, a red light pulsing, my own personal siren blaring. The police car means danger. I don't think, because I don't have time to think, but I see pictures in my mind. They're only there for a split second, but the pictures make my insides squelch like the sound of a bootprint in soft mud.

The first picture is of Bernard standing in his office

155

with the policemen, waiting for me. He must have asked to see me in his room, not because he wanted to talk to me, but because he'd asked the police to come and interrogate me instead. They could be looking for me now, waiting to take me in. The second picture is of the velvet box. I remember picking up the box on Kent's desk and opening it to peep inside; it'll be covered with my fingerprints. So will the watch because I picked that up as well. The watch will have my fingerprints on the sides and on the back. The last picture is of a policewoman climbing the stairs to my room to try and find me. I imagine her knocking on the door, then opening it and finding my case half-packed inside. I turn around and run.

I run back along the path, beneath the trees. When it crosses the dirt track leading up the mound, I stop motionless and listen. I check there's no one coming before I dash across, around the corner and through the field. I'm going to the farm. I can feel the rain streaming down my face, my nose is running with the cold but I don't have time to stop and find a hankie. I have to find somewhere to hide.

I open the farmyard gate and step across the puddles in the courtyard. I fumble with the catch on the door, then open it and stumble inside the little stable where the goats live. I close the door behind me so nobody knows I'm here, then I crawl across the piles of straw and huddle into a corner in the dark.

I want to sit down and recover. I want to find time to think. I want to reassess what's happening; I need time to be quiet on my own.

The hairy monkey is still clawing its way around the inside of my stomach. I don't know what I'm going to do with it. Its claws are scraping at me, trying to tell me something. I think the monkey is feeling claustrophobic. It needs to get out and breathe.

I curl up with my arms around my knees, hidden in my nest of straw, listening to the wind blow and the rain pouring down outside. At least I'm dry.

And then, there's a rustling in the straw. It makes me jump at first, but of course I know what it is. I'd forgotten there would be animals here as well. They need to shelter from the rain.

The straw beside me parts and Sheba's nose comes nuzzling through to nibble at my drenched clothing. She thinks I'm here to feed them. Then the baby goats stumble over and start mouthing their way all round me. They stick their noses in my armpits and under my knees and behind my ears, searching for their feeding bottles. Then they start nibbling at my mac. I put my hands round the neck of one of the baby goats and stroke its head and throat. I start to fondle its ears.

"I haven't brought any milk for you," I start to explain, but I find that my voice is sobbing.

"I'm sorry, I..." but I can't say any more because my throat is thick with hair. The monkey is there inside my throat, reaching out its claws, trying to get some fresh air. I start to cough and choke. I wrap my arms tightly round the baby goat and I lean against its soft, warm, hairy skin. Then I start to sob. Tears pour out of my eyes like the underground river in the little village, gurgling to the surface. The baby kid doesn't move away; it stays there patiently like a soft cushion and lets my tears stream on to its neck.

The fear rolls out, down on to the goat. The sadness. The disappointment, washed out with the tears, soaking the goat's soft skin.

And then the monkey comes out, crawling like a giant

157

spider, hairy in my throat and then sticking out his furry head and squawking. I think the monkey is made of hatred because, when I feel it rising up inside me, I think about Kent Wilkinson. I think about how I hate him. Everything is his fault. If it wasn't for him, I'd be working at Castle Head now, cooking the supper and making the log fires and feeling accepted - everything I wanted to be, part of the Castle Head family.

I think about the conversation that I overheard when I was sitting outside the wall. The boys said they were going across the bay and returning late at night. They could be sucked down in the quicksands; they could drown when the tide comes in. I imagine their bodies washed up on the beach somewhere, purple and bloated and dead. And I feel a little surge of pleasure, like when I saw Kent Wilkinson, posing on the staircase, and I wanted him to fall. That's what I want to happen now; I want bad things to happen to him so that I can get my own back. I know I ought to tell Bernard or one of their stupid teachers about them crossing the sands at night, but I shan't. It's their own fault for being so idiotic. I'd feel happier if they drown. I might get my inheritance back then.

There's a soft nuzzling at my side. Sheba has returned. In the semi-darkness, I can see the soft pools of her eyes, gazing at me questioningly. She brings her head close to mine, so that I can feel her soft breath on my face and then, very very gently, she starts to lick my face. Her tongue is bumpy and ticklish; it scrapes against my skin like warm, wet denim, but Sheba licks my tears away. Slowly, gently, rhythmically, one tear at a time.

The smell of the goats is everywhere; the whole place smells of animal, of milk and straw and hay. And I feel suddenly comforted. Here I am, wrapped in the straw like a little nest, licked better by a goat and I want to just collapse. I want to be helpless. I don't want any responsibility. I wish I could be a goat. I just want to feel protected and looked after. I want somebody to care about me. Because nobody does, of course. It doesn't matter to anyone if I lose my job and get sent to prison for something I haven't done. Nobody is bothered. I don't even think Sheba and her kids would miss me.

I will love her, of course.

When I discovered that my baby was a little girl, well, I thought that he might die with the disappointment of it. His hopes had been so high. He wanted a son to rule Castle Head and all the land and farming. A son who would understand the ways of steam engines. A son who would carry on as his father had, after his father was dead.

Of course I will love my little girl. She will be a friend to me. She will stay close by my side and I shall teach her how to read and write, how to milk the cows and cut the wool off sheep. She will not leave me to go away and learn about the workings of a steam engine.

But then of course, he insists that all is not yet lost. It is hard to believe - a man of his age, but he is so determined. I think there is no stopping him. If I would not agree, then I think he would consider someone else.

And now I have a child, my name is written in his will. I shall inherit from him and so shall my children after. The name of Lewis shall go on and none of us will be poor. And that is how it should be, for how can I be a servant again when I have lain in a bed with my master? How can I sit at the below stairs table in the position of the meek and lowly after we have shared so much together?

I may not be a lady yet, but I think I might quickly learn.

"Well, it's a good job they sent a whole packet of these Tiggiwinkle wigs," says Cartmel, using one to wipe the steamed-up windows of the Cumbrian TV van. "They've come in really useful."

Members of the film crew have been using the wigs as ear mufflers to keep out the howling wind which has swept across Morecambe Bay for most of the day. Others have used them as cushions when they've needed to sit on a wet rock to take a low-angled shot. They've also used them as dusters and as camera lens-shields, and the boy who took their order to the Golden Dragon fish and chip shop, used three folded together to keep their chips warm until he got back.

Humphrey sits disconsolately in the van, in his Feel Me Slowly cowboy hat, watching the rain streaming down the windows.

"Are you sure you won't have any chips, Humphrey?" Cartmel asks. "Or would you like some of my rissole?"

Humphrey thinks about his friends in London who would now be meeting in their local wine bar, sampling the gastronomic delights specially prepared by Marcel, the resident French chef.

"You could dip the chips in some curry sauce..."

Humphrey shakes his head in dismay. The rain has soaked through his jacket, through his shirt and even through his thermal vest. His feet are wet, his assorted toupés have all been used as dusters, and his brandy flask is empty.

"Do you think we'll be able to finish shooting this afternoon?" Lin asks him.

The main problem is the giant hedgehog. Even without its white lace pinafore and wearing a blonde wig, it still looks like a hedgehog. It seems to be the sharp pointed nose, the claws on the end of its paws, and its hundreds of prickles that give the game away. However hard they've tried, nobody can make the hedgehog look anything like Lin Dale.

"I think it's brightening up," chirps Cartmel.

What she means is that the rain isn't quite as heavy as it was a few seconds before.

The chief cameraman wipes a circle of steam away from the nearest window. "Do you think we can try the helicopter again?" he asks Humphrey. "See if they can get that hedgehog out of the way."

Once Humphrey decided they would have to manage without the long shots of the figure drowning in the sands, they then found it impossible to film without the giant hedgehog creeping into shot. The model had become firmly implanted in the sands and only a helicopter was strong enough to winch it out.

"I don't think they'll want to risk it," says Cartmel, "not in this weather. The pilot said they'd only come out again in an emergency."

Humphrey takes a deep breath and goes red in the face. "Well, if this isn't an emergency," he storms, "I'd like to know what is." He screws up an empty chip bag and slings it across the van. "We're supposed to finish the shooting today; we're cold and wet; the video is turning into a disaster movie and every shot we take is dominated by a giant bloody hedgehog!"

161

Twenty Four

Drrrrr. Drrrrrr.

  Drrrrr. Drrrrrr.

"Hello. Guides Farm."

"Hello. Is that Cedric Robinson?"

"Speaking."

"Oh, hello Cedric. It's Pat Lambert here from the greengrocer's. I wanted to tell you about this...I've seen this kind of....well, I suppose it must be a...it seems like a person, really, stuck out in the sands."

"Oh dear. Whereabouts?"

"Down towards the Channel."

"Good gracious me. That's a long way. Can you see them from the shore?"

"Mmmm. It's a very big person, actually; it seems larger than normal. You can see her blonde hair and, well ...a rather pointed face."

"Oh. What do you think she's doing?"

"Well, she isn't moving at all. That's why, that's why I thought she was stuck. That's what made me think I'd better phone you."

"Isn't she waving her arms or anything."

"No...it's, she's er...it's just completely still. It's strange really."

"Can you hold on a minute. I'll go out to the telescope and have a look."

Cedric focusses his telescope and pans it across the bay. He sees empty sand and occasional seabirds. Then he finds the channel and then a large blob. He focusses the lens more keenly. The edges of the blob begin to sharpen. The colours appear more strongly. There certainly seems to be the figure of a woman. A tall and rather plump lady, wearing a long dress and a white frilly pinafore. Cedric frowns. This is most unusual, hardly suitable clothing for wearing out on the bay. He's always telling people that they should go out suitably dressed. He trains the telescope up and down the figure. She certainly has a mop of blonde hair, but when his telescope focusses on her face, he gasps aloud with shock. She seems to have a head of spikes. But when he sees her face in detail, Cedric cannot believe his eyes. Here in front of him, out in the bay, is an outrageously-dressed giant hedgehog, sinking down into the sand.

I open my eyes and, at first, I don't know where I am. The sun is beating on my face, so I know I'm not indoors. I can hear birds singing. I look round and find I'm in the little stable where the goats live. I must have fallen asleep.

Now, it's like a new day. The rain has stopped and the sun is sparkling on the puddles. I can hear water dripping from the roof and from the big trees round the farm. There's a warm steaminess of damp straw, heated by the sun. The goats have left me and are outside in the sunshine. It must nearly be time for their supper.

I stand up and my legs are stiff. I don't know how long I've been asleep. I reach out my hand to the wall for support and then I start to remember what I'm doing in here with the goats, and my stomach sinks. I was trying to escape, wanting to run away and hide, but now I know I can't do that. I've got to go back and clear up the mess. I haven't stolen Kent Wilkinson's watch, but no one else knows that apart from me. I've got to go back and tell them. I must explain to Bernard. Otherwise, what will he think if he sees my half-packed case?

I walk out into the fresh air and sunshine. I'm feeling better now. Perhaps a good cry and a little sleep have done me good. The goats come nuzzling round me, but this time I think it's because they're hungry; I wonder why they've not been fed. I set off back to Castle Head.

The sun is shining on my back as I walk up the lane towards the house. I'll go in the front door this time. I'll walk in the front door and go straight to Bernard's office and explain. I'll tell him how I only went in Kent's room to turn off his tape recorder. I'll explain that I was scared because I thought they might suspect me of stealing his watch. Bernard might understand. They might even have found the watch by now. That's the thought that cheers me up as I walk up the steps to the house.

Inside, everything is quiet. I listen for the sound of conversation or for a radio playing somewhere, but I can't hear anything at all. I look in the library, but there's no one there. I walk down to Bernard's office. The door is open but the office is empty. I wonder where everyone is.

I wander down into the kitchen. Supper is over and everything has been washed up and tidied away. I feel a bit hungry now. I might come down and make myself a sandwich later.

But, still there's no one about; no one at all. I listen again. There ought to be voices or a radio somewhere. I walk up the other staircase to the rooms where the boys are staying, but there's no sign of them. I start to feel a bit uneasy. Where did I hear the boys say they were going? To a concert? That's right. A concert across the bay. I remember the conversation that I overheard. "Bring your buckets and spades," said Kent. "We'll stop and make some sandcastles." I have a horrible sinking slump of guilt. I should have told Bernard straightaway. They mustn't try to come back on their own. They could die in the quicksands at night. No one must cross the bay without the guide. And I don't think Cedric Robinson would be too happy about being knocked up at midnight to bring a bunch of lager louts home from a rock concert. But what if they've already gone? What if it's too late? I don't know what to do now.

I walk down the corridor to my room. I think perhaps I'll make a cup of tea and have a think, but then as I approach my door, I see the envelope. It's pinned on the outside of my door with my name in big block letters:

JENNY
URGENT!

My insides sink like a lead coffin in the quicksand.

Twenty five

Drrrrr. Drrrrrr.

Drrrrr. Drrrrrr.

"Hello. Guides Farm."

"Hello. Is that Cedric Robinson?"

"Speaking."

"Hello Cedric. It's Bob here from the garage. I've just seen this figure stuck out in the bay. I think she must be in distress. It looks like an old woman. She seems to be wearing a long dress. I wonder if you could go across and try to help her..."

"She's not over towards the Channel, is she?"

"That's right. Has someone already phoned you?"

Cedric sighs. "Look, it's nothing to worry about. It's Cumbrian TV. They were using this model in their filming and then they couldn't pull her out of the sands. They were going to hire a helicopter but the weather was too bad. They've decided to leave the model there until tomorrow."

"Oh, well, that's a relief. I thought it might be somebody in trouble."

"No, no. Don't worry. It's a giant hedgehog, actually."

"I thought she had a rather pointed nose."

"Mmm. Well, I don't know what they've been using it for."

"It's probably some new-fangled soap opera. Right, well I'm sorry to have troubled you, anyway."

"Not at all. It's always best to be on the safe side."

"Well, that's what I thought."

"Better to have twenty false alarms than leave somebody to drown."

"Well, I agree. Anyway, I'll let you get on with your work. Bye, Cedric."

"Goodbye."

Dear Jenny,

I've gone out in the police car to help them look for the old woman who was round here. I'm certain she's the one who stole Kent's watch, but now she's disappeared. Penny has gone to visit her sister and it's Alli's night off so I'm leaving you in charge for a few hours. I'm sorry to lumber you with this, but it is an emergency. I'm worried that old lady might do something stupid. She didn't seem to be quite in her right mind to me.

The animals need feeding at seven o'clock, but I might be back before then. I'll phone up later and check that everything's okay.

The two teachers went out earlier on but they said they were going bird-watching so they should be back before it gets dark. I think the boys were going out somewhere for the evening as well, so you shouldn't have to worry about them.

Bernard.

P.S. I forgot to thank you for doing the slides last night. I was very grateful and I'm sorry I seem to have left them in such a mess.

I look at the time. It's eight o'clock. No wonder the animals looked hungry.

I've been left in charge and I've made a right mess of it so far. What if Bernard comes back and finds the animals starving to death? I put the milk on for their bottles and try to sort things out.

I've been really stupid today. Nobody ever thought I'd

taken the watch at all; they assumed that it was the mad woman. Of course, I remember now. I saw her walking by the river with her sack, just before Kent noticed that the watch was missing. I'd forgotten all about that. I'll have to tell the police. I don't know why it never occurred to me before that it might be her. So the police hadn't come to arrest me after all; Bernard had sent for them to find where the mad woman had hobbled off to. They must need him to identify her and to identify the watch. I had all that worry for nothing.

I decide to fill all six bottles and take them out together. I don't know if I can feed six assorted goats and sheep at once but I can try.

I feel a lot happier now. Bernard doesn't think I'm a criminal and he doesn't even think it was my fault that the slides were mixed-up. He must have decided that I'm quite sensible to leave me in charge of Castle Head. I hope he doesn't come back before the animals are fed.

The lambs and kids charge forwards like teenagers waiting outside all day for tickets to a pop concert. I brace myself against the wall, but they still almost knock me over. I'm in danger of being buried in open, salivating mouths, chewing on my coat and on my legs and nosing inside my wellies. The goats stand on their hind legs and try to climb up me to grab the bottles from my hand, but I hold my ground. I lock the teat of one bottle into a lamb's grasping mouth and then, when it starts to suck, I transfer the bottle in between my knees, pull a second bottle out of my pocket, fasten a kid on the end of that, transfer that between my legs as well and then manage to feed the others somehow with two bottles in each hand. I feel ridiculous. I don't know what I must look like.

The lambs' tails are wagging ninety to the dozen, and

168

the air is filled with the gluggings of contentment. And this is all I ever want, you see. I just want to be here, at Castle Head, me and all the animals. I want it to last for ever. I want to be able to feed and look after all the animals and have people here who rely on me and trust me and don't mind leaving me in charge.

I think about Kent Wilkinson and his disappointment about his jetski and his watch. I wouldn't even want a jetski; I wouldn't know what to do with one. Just give me a contented lamb. I'd swap that for a car with foggy windows and all the money Kent's family has inside the bank.

And then I start to think again about the inheritance. About Anne Lewis and John Wilkinson. It had occurred to me before that, if Kent were to drown in the quicksands, it might be possible for me to inherit all the money. If I really were descended from Anne Lewis, then perhaps I could prove it somehow and all the money would be mine.

But I'm not so sure about that. My mum used to say that sometimes I let my imagination run away with me. Like the fairy tale I dreamed about my real father being a pop star and showering me with presents. Life's not like that. Things like that don't happen. Even if I do believe I might be descended from Ann Lewis, I don't think I could prove it. So why should anyone believe me? And even if I could prove it, I wouldn't get the money if Kent died; it would just go to his parents or to his brother or sister. And, of course, I wouldn't want it anyway. I wouldn't want to have to talk in a ridiculous accent and be driven about by a chauffeur. I wouldn't want to go to an expensive boarding school where all you ever learned was selfishness. I'd rather be in the stable in my wellies with the goats.

The bottles are almost finished now. I have to tip them right up so the animals can drain them. And I remember someone saying: It isn't where you come from; it's who you are that counts. Someone said it recently; I can't remember where. And I have a sudden nice thought about myself: I don't know where I come from. I don't even know who my real parents are. I don't know who my proper grandparents are. I thought it really mattered, where I came from. That's why I've been trying to find out. But perhaps it isn't really so important. Why should I be spending all my time trying to prove things about my past? It's who I am now that counts. I grin to myself. I think I'm quite a nice person really. I know I'm not very clever but I don't think that's important. I care about the animals.

"No more now," I say to the lambs that are trying to chew up the empty bottles. "Come on; you've had enough."

I put the empty bottles in my coat pockets and I pat and stroke the lambs and kids. I must set off back now and go and look after things at Castle Head. I must be responsible now that I'm in charge.

Twenty six

Drrrrr. Drrrrrr.

Drrrrr. Drrrrrr.

"Hello. Guides Farm."

"Hello there. Is that you, Cedric?"

"Speaking."

"Oh, Cedric, it's John Patterson here, from the news-agents. I wanted to tell you about this...I've seen this lady...well, I suppose it must be a...well, it seems like a very large person, stuck out..."

"It's all right. Don't worry," Cedric interrupts. "We already know about it. It's some idiots at Cumbrian TV that've left it there. It's only a model."

"Oh, I'm sorry, I was just..."

"We've been getting phone calls about it all night long."

"Well, I didn't want to..."

"I told them not to go out there in the first place. They're a load of total wallies. They're about as much use as an ashtray on a jetski."

"Mmm, well, I..."

"Next time I see that idiot film director, I'll give him a piece of my mind."

"Right, well, I er..."

"I daren't take the phone off the hook in case there's a real emergency."

"Well, I quite understand, Cedric. I'll leave you in peace. Good night."

"Good night."

I walk back to Castle Head and the phone is ringing. I hope it's Bernard.

I run into the office, plonk several dirty feeding bottles down on Bernard's in-tray and pick up the phone.

"Hello, Castle Head? I wonder if I could make a booking?"

I'm tempted to say no and ask her to phone back when there's somebody sensible here, but then I remember that I'm supposed to be sensible and in charge so I look at the calendar on the wall and tell this person when there's a week-end with two spare rooms. "Perhaps you could write and confirm," I ask her, "and send us a deposit?"

"Yes, of course."

I write down all the particulars, then go downstairs to make a cup of tea.

I remember next that I haven't eaten, so I inspect the contents of the fridge and grill myself a cheese muffin. Then I sit down with my food and cup of tea and have a think. I don't seem to think too well on an empty stomach.

I wish Bernard would phone.

I don't know what to do about Kent and his friends coming back late tonight. Now I'm in charge, I have to be responsible. And it's not enough just to care about the animals. You have to care about people as well. People are really more important.

The person I ought to talk to is Bernard. I hope he comes back soon.

Perhaps I could phone the police but then, I'm not certain whether there's any real danger or not. I'd feel really stupid, getting all the police cars out if, all the time, the boys were sitting in the pub down in the village. They might have changed their minds about the concert when the weather was so bad this afternoon.

I finish off my muffin and swill it down with tea. I could nip down to the pub - that would take me, what? Half an hour to go there and back? But then I think of Bernard coming home and finding the place empty. Or he might phone whilst I was out and wonder where I'd gone. I don't know what to do.

I make myself another cup of tea.

If only I'd spoken to Bernard earlier this afternoon. If I'd told him about the conversation that I'd heard, sitting on the seat...he could have called the boys in and spoken to them...he could have told Dr Lune and Marjorie, then none of this would have happened...

I have a drink of my tea and then I think of something else. I could phone Cedric Robinson. He could tell me whether the tide will be out or not later on tonight. Perhaps he could advise me what to do.

I take my tea upstairs and find a phone directory in the office. I look up Robinson, C. I feel a bit stupid. I hope Cedric won't think I'm just wasting his time. I rehearse what I'm going to say before I dial: Hello, Mr Robinson, it's Jenny Brown here from Castle Head. You don't know me. I'm very sorry to trouble you. I wanted to speak to you about somebody going out on the quicksands...

The line's engaged. I'll try again later.

Humphrey wonders about the wig.

He drinks a glass of brandy as he looks out of his hotel window and notices that the sun is shining, the rain has stopped and the tide is out.

The film crew are drinking in the downstairs bar, but Humphrey doesn't want to join them. He isn't in the mood for celebrating. All he wants to do is leave this uncultured dump of a place and rejoin his friends in their London wine bar. He wonders what Marcel will be cooking for Saturday lunch. Escargot, perhaps? Coq au vin? He must get back in time.

But the problem, of course, is the wig. He can't turn up at the wine bar completely bald. And his Feel me Slowly hat would hardly seem appropriate. But the wig on Mrs Tiggiwinkle...that would be perfect...just his style. The colour was a little brash, but...he could always tell people he'd been filming in the Mediterranean and the sun had bleached his hair...

Humphrey pours himself another brandy and looks at the sink in the corner of his room. He can wash the wig and dry it on the radiator. He has some shampoo and a bottle of conditioner. It would need to be washed, of course. The wig could be covered in seagull droppings by now or even shreds of seaweed.

Humphrey can see the bay, dry and empty as a desert now that the tide is out. The hedgehog isn't too far away. There isn't much danger of the wig having blown away because it's impaled quite firmly on the hedgehog spines and, anyway, he'd taken the precaution of fastening it down with the sticky Kiss me Quick label from his hat. He grins to himself. No one need know where he is. He can have a pleasant walk out along the beach. An evening stroll. No one will be any wiser.

He fills up his hip flask with brandy, puts on his leather jacket and his Feel me Slowly hat and walks down to the hotel foyer. Then he strolls into the early summer sunset down towards the beach, proud of the fact that not a single person knows where he is going.

Twenty seven

Drrrrr. Drrrrrr.

 Drrrrr. Drrrrrr.

 "Hello. Guides Farm."

 "Hello there. Is that you, Cedric?"

 "Speaking."

 "Oh, Cedric, it's John here, from The Vicarage. I thought I ought to tell you about this...I've seen this sort of...well, I suppose it must be a very large person, stuck out..."

Cedric holds the receiver at arm's length and says a very rude word.

 "Sorry, Cedric. I didn't quite catch you..."

Cedric takes a deep breath.

 "She doesn't seem to be moving at all. She must be suffering from exhaustion. I think it must be a tourist, Cedric. She doesn't look dressed for hiking across the sands."

Cedric tries very hard to keep calm. He speaks very slowly to the Reverend Jones from The Vicarage because he knows that, if he isn't careful, he's in danger of losing his temper.

 "It is not a lady in distress," he explains. "It is a giant hedgehog. A hedgehog covered in spines and wearing a white pinafore and a blonde wig. It is not in distress at all because it has no feelings. I, on the other hand, Cedric Robinson, do have feelings. I am sick to death about having to answer the phone every few minutes for a ruddy hedgehog. I have had enough. I am a fisherman and a guide across the sands. I am not a hedgehog

175

keeper and I don't like hedgehogs anyway. I am going out now with my chainsaw to saw its bloody head off."

With that, Cedric puts down the telephone. He finds his wellington boots and waterproofs then goes out to his tractor and hitches it up to the trailer with his chain saw on the back.

I try Cedric's number again but it's still engaged. I try to keep calm. I have to do something sensible. On the table is a little booklet which tells you the times of the high and low tides. What I need is some idea of what time the concert ends and when the tide comes in. Once I've found that out, I'll know whether there's really any danger.

I look up today's date in the little yellow book. The times it gives are for Barrow in Furness but that isn't far away. I think the tides will be about the same round here. This Friday, high tide is at 23.50 - that's ten to twelve. Add an hour for British Summer Time makes ten to one. If they set off back late in the evening, the sands might seem safe, but the tide will be rushing in. It'll certainly be high tide before they've had time to walk across.

I try Cedric's number again but it's still engaged. I hope he hasn't left his phone off the hook. I think I'll have to walk to the pub in the village and see if the boys are there. If Kent and his friends really have gone to the concert then I might have to phone the police. I just wish I'd done something about it earlier. I feel so stupid.

I find a writing pad and a biro in the office and leave a note:

Dear Bernard
I am very worried about some of the Belmount

*boys who I think have gone out to a pop concert
across the bay. I'm just going to check they're not
in the local pub before I get into a real panic about
them.
I'll come straight back.
I'm sorry I missed you this afternoon. I hope
you've found the watch.
Love
Jenny.*

*   *   *

*By night; by day;
Alu La Lay...*

A lone figure in the early sunset, Rhiannon places her
jumbo on the sands. She stands on the smooth wooden
board and grasps the handles at the sides, then she rocks
gently backwards and forwards.

*By night; by day;
Alu La Lay
Alu Rhiannon...*

She rocks rhythmically, to and fro, with the satisfaction
of an old woman sitting in her rocking chair by the fire.

Alu La Lay...

As she rocks, she sees the dimples in the sand as the
cockle shells are brought up to the surface. Then she
stops. She steps off the jumbo and takes the short rake
from out of her sack. With long, regular movements, she
scratches the cockles out of the sand and sweeps them

towards her. Her arms are strong and muscular. She rakes the cockles with the easy movement of an old woman sweeping her cottage floor. Then she opens her sack. She folds down the top, pleating it over into a circular nest. She bends down and lifts up the small shells in her hands but, as she places them inside her sack, she notices something round and glistening. The fading summer sunshine flashes on something hard and metallic. Puzzled, Rhiannon puts down the cockles then takes the watch out of her sack.

"Here we go, here we go, here we go.Here we go, here we go, here we go.o.o.o...

"Do you fancy some of this curry sauce, Arnold? There seems to be rather more sauce than curry here."

"No, I'm fine, thanks. It doesn't go too well with the fried haddock."

"How about you Warton? Want some curry on your cockles?"

"No thanks, Kent. I'm fine."

"Well, it's a jolly good night for a stroll, eh what? Full moon..."

"Ho..o...o...w...w...l. Ho..o...o...w...w...l..."

Ho..o...o...w...w...l. "

"Miles of bare sand..."

"It's just like the desert."

"I say, if you drive a Lada in the desert, why is it compulsory to have a stereo system?"

"I don't know, Kent. Why is it compulsory to have a stereo system if you drive a Lada in the desert?"

"So you don't go mad with boredom while you're waiting for the breakdown truck!"

"Ha, ha very funny."

"I say, Kent, did you check what time high tide is

tonight?"

"No, never bothered."

"You said you were going to find out."

"I asked Warton to do it, didn't I? What time's high tide, Warton?"

"Twelve hours after low tide."

"There you are, you see. Twelve hours after low tide. Satisfied?"

"Well, we want to know who to blame if we drown."

"I'll tell you what, Arnold...we'll have a bet on it. A thousand pounds. If we all drown, I owe you a thousand; if we don't, you owe me a thousand. All right?"

"I'll have to think about that, Kent. Pass some lager over. It's thirsty work, walking across the desert."

"Ho..o...o...w...w...l...."

Twenty eight

I run back to Castle Head. As I turn off the main road and into the drive, I take my torch out of my pocket. I switch it on, even though I can see the pathway shining in the moonlight. I can see my way very clearly, but I keep the torch on for some comfort.

A rabbit scampers into the hedgerow, but I don't have time to stand and look at rabbits. I want to get back now and phone the police. I should have done that hours ago. Now it might be too late.

I pull up the collar on my mac as the wind whistles down my neck. It will be cold now, out on the bay. The tide will be coming in.

I try to keep jogging, even though I'm out of breath. I never was very good at running. An owl swoops past from one of the big trees on my right, but I can watch owls any time. I think every second counts now. I have to get back and ask for help.

I'll try Cedric Robinson first, but if he's not in I'll phone the police. I just can't believe why I didn't do this earlier.

At least I have more information now. The little boy, Sandy, the one who wears a tie, told me that he'd overheard Kent and Arnold making plans. "They arranged to meet at the Golden Dragon," he explained. "I think it's a chip shop on the other side of the bay. That was just in case they lost each other at the concert. They were going to meet there at quarter to ten to set off back."

But of course, it's after that now. They should already

be walking back across the sands. But walking back on a route they don't know, without even Cedric's brods to guide them and walking back with the tide racing in, silently behind them.

The house is quiet and there are no cars parked outside. I pull off my boots and then run straight up to Bernard's office. I can take off my mac whilst I'm on the phone. I have to look up Cedric's number again in the directory because I haven't written it down. I try to stop my hand shaking whilst I dial the number. The phone rings. At least it's not engaged.

I don't know how long to leave it. Cedric might be outside in his shed or settling his hens down for the night. I wish he'd hurry up. I notice a couple of empty feeding bottles that I've left in Bernard's in-tray. I must take them downstairs afterwards and wash them. Perhaps I've dialed the wrong number. I replace the receiver, dial again then let it ring twelve times. Whilst the phone's ringing, I take off my coat.

It's no good. I let the phone ring another three times then I find the number of the police station. Perhaps Bernard will be there. I'd feel better if I could talk to him.

"Hello, Grange Police. Desk Sergeant Whiting here. Can I help you?"

"Hello, my name's Jenny Brown from Castle Head Field Studies Centre. I'm worried about somebody trying to cross the bay at night. I think they might get cut off by the tide."

"Look, if it's this hedgehog you're on about, we've just about had enough. We've been having calls all night and it's getting beyond a joke."

Hedgehog? I feel sure he said hedgehog. I must have made a mistake. "I was thinking they might drown when the tide comes in," I explain.

"The first few calls weren't so bad but now it's got ridiculous. We can't do anything about Mrs Tiggiwinkle till low tide."

It sounded like hedgehog. I try to think of other words that sound similar...fresh bog? Dead frog? None of them make sense. I'm sure he said hedgehog. And Mrs. Tiggiwinkle.

"Hello...are you still there?"

"Yes, I, er... I wondered if I could speak to Mr Wharfe, Bernard Wharfe, from Castle Head. I understand he's helping you with your enquiries."

"Just one moment please."

Mrs Tiggiwinkle is a character in a book. I'm sure she is. Unless she's a famous local resident. I don't know what to think.

"Hello."

"Hello."

"Are you still there?"

I try not to sigh too loudly. "Yes."

"Mr Wharfe's on his way back to Castle Head. He said he'd left a young girl there in charge and it wasn't really fair on her. He should be back in a couple of minutes time."

"All right. Thank you very much."

"Goodbye."

"Bye."

I take the feeding bottles downstairs to wash up and put the kettle on to make a cup of tea for Bernard and myself. I'll let him talk to the police instead.

Rhiannon peers quizzically in the moonlight at the iron bridge and its reflection in the river. The iron circle. Tiny jewels, set into the golden casing, sparkle as she swings the watch to and fro. The picture seems to evoke a distant memory, something long-forgotten, like a place once visited in early childhood. She weighs the watch in her hand, and again, there is something familiar about the shape and about its heaviness even though, at first, she cannot quite remember where she has seen the watch before and how it came to be in her possession.

Although she cannot see the detail in the moonlight, her memory evokes the delicately-painted picture of a wooded valley. Through her mind's eye, Rhiannon can recall the branches on the trees and the small bird perched upon a branch. She can feel the spot where the tiny initials are inscribed on the bottom: J.W.

Her coarse, gnarled fingers stroke the gold at the back of the watch, tracing out a pattern, a pattern of scrolls and linking circles, an ancient design. Her calloused fingers follow the curves: the end of one is the beginning of the next. As one man dies, another is born. A civilization dies and another one grows from its ashes.

Rhiannon turns the watch over. She brings it back close to her eyes, to peer in the moonlight at a snarling serpent, swallowing the tail of another serpent, swallowing the tail of yet another. Her eyes begin to widen with the dawn of recognition. "An evil sign," she murmurs. "I told him it was an evil sign."

She stands, gazing into the moonlight, pondering the meaning of the serpents. They have snarling eyes and lashing tails; they continuously eat each other: snarling and swallowing; swallowing and snarling. Someone has to break the circle. Someone has to break the force of evil. The snarling serpents have to be destroyed.

Rhiannon raises her arm as if to throw the watch onto the beach, but then she pauses. The tide will come in and then go out again, ebbing and flowing like the serpents. She must throw the serpents in deep water, in the quicksands. They must not be left beached at low tide for someone else to find.

Carefully, Rhiannon places the watch inside her folded sack. She covers the watch and the cockles with her jumbo, then she fastens the sack around the neck and lifts it up high on her shoulder. She looks ahead. She will just have time to reach the channel before the tide comes in. She will have to hurry.

"Here we slide, here we slide, here we slide..."

"It's not funny any longer, Kent; it's getting dangerous."

"Oh, rubbish, old chap. Just a bit of wet sand. No prob. Be through it in a couple of ticks."

"You can feel it pulling on your feet. I don't think we ought to stand still."

"Well, we won't do, will we? We'll make for that rock thing over there, look. Then we'll sit down and polish off the lager."

"What rock? There aren't any rocks surely, not in the middle of the beach?"

"Well, there's something over there. What do you think, Warton? Ocean-going Lada? Gets 2 kilometres out to sea then needs a new engine?"

"I think the tide's coming in."

"Rubbish!"

"Well, it's getting wetter."

"Don't you think we ought to go back, Arnold?"

"Well, how long's it taken us so far? An hour and a half? We must be near the other side now."

"I'm getting worried."

"You know, I think it looks more like a person."

"What's that Warton?"

"That shape over there. It looks like somebody standing still. It might be a fisherman. What do you think, Kent?"

"Mmm. Funny shape. Looks more like an old woman. She's probably the deckchair attendant."

"Look Kent, it's not funny any more. We're getting wetter every minute. We could drown out here. And it was all your stupid idea in the first place."

"You didn't have to come."

"Well, you said you'd check the times of the tides and you never bothered."

"Look you've been to see The Celtic Dead haven't you? You'd never have seen them live if it wasn't for me."

"The only person I want to see live now is me. And the chances of that are getting slimmer."

"Okay then, look, we'll head towards the old fisherwoman. She must know the way. We'll just have to cross this bit of water..."

"Bit of water! It'll be up to my chest!"

"I don't know whether we can cross there, Kent. There might be a current."

"What do you want to do, then? Go back?"

"We can't go back; it's too far. We must be more than halfway now."

"Okay then, I'll go first as I'm the tallest. If you see me disappear, then you'll know it's too deep. And I'll carry the lager on my head. We don't want to lose that. We might need something to drink while we're waiting for the tide to go back out."

Cedric Robinson drives his tractor across the sands. Normally, he wouldn't go on the beach when the tide is coming in but tonight he is determined to saw the top off

Mrs Tiggiwinkle. He cannot possibly cope with a whole night of phone calls from people wanting him to go out and rescue her.

It shouldn't take long to saw the hedgehog in half. He parks his tractor on a nearby stretch of firm sand, then takes his chainsaw out of the trailer. He gives a couple of practice whirrs on the trigger to check that it's working all right then carries it across the sand.

As Cedric walks nearer, he surveys the shape in front of him. He was assuming that Mrs Tiggiwinkle would have feet, or paws anyway; all she seems to have is a skirt. The only narrow part seems to be round her waist. It shouldn't matter if there's a stump left in the sand, so long as most of her is invisible by the time he's finished with the chainsaw.

Twenty nine

"No sign of anyone over there."

The police car keeps stopping and we get out and look across the bay. I think it's hopeless. I don't think we'll find them now. I feel weak and hollow because I know it's my fault. I should have told Bernard earlier on, as soon as I heard them talking. And all I did was cry myself to sleep, sitting with the goats. I shall never forgive myself.

"We'd better go round to the chip shop then. See 'f anyone there can remember them."

The police want to check that the boys really have set out across the bay before they get anyone else out on the search. They find it hard to believe that the boys could be so stupid. Especially when I told them they were sixteen and went to a posh boarding school."

We drive on towards the village. I've been thinking all the time about why I didn't tell anyone earlier. I do know why it was. It was because I felt so hurt. I thought I was going to lose my job and I thought I might be blamed for stealing Kent's watch and I felt angry. I thought everything was his fault. It was the anger that was bubbling up inside me, the hairy monkey; that was what made me want to hurt him - to get my own back. For a tiny fraction of a second, I actually wanted him to die.

The Golden Dragon is closed. I wait in the car whilst the policemen walk round the back of the shop to get the owner out of bed.

And I wonder if it might be the same with other people. You see, I've always assumed that it's the people who are powerful and nasty who do the greatest damage, but now I'm wondering. I'm not powerful and nasty; I'm fairly harmless really, but for a tiny fraction of a second, I actually wanted Kent to die. I wonder if murderers are like that. I wonder if they might only mean someone harm for a second and then regret it the rest of their lives. I wonder if evil goes round in circles so that, if someone hurts you, you want to hurt them back. And if you can't, you try to hurt someone else. Perhaps it's the powerless and weak who do the greatest damage. It's not the ghosts, but the people who think they're being haunted.

I can see the lights going on in the chip shop. The owner is getting out of bed.

If evil does go round in circles, then when someone hurts you, it makes you want to hurt someone else; when someone bites you, you bite someone else. Like a ring of serpents, each one swallowing another's tail.

The first policeman runs back to the car. He sits down quickly and picks up his radio. "They remembered the lads," he tells me. "They left here nearly two hours ago."

He speaks into his radio. "Hello. Sergeant Whiting here. Can you get me the coastguard please."

The second policeman is still talking to the chip shop man. I think he's Chinese. He's standing on the doorstep in his dressing gown.

Sergeant Whiting looks anxiously out of the window towards the bay. "Let's hope we're in time," he says to me. "The tide'll be in very soon."

Cedric raises the chainsaw on a level with his hip like a cowboy striding to the shoot-out. As he approaches Mrs Tiggiwinkle, he presses the trigger which whirrs the saw into motion.

"Aaaaaaaaaaaaaaaaaaagh!!!"

Cedric stops, horrified. The scream is coming from the hedgehog.

"Aaaaaaaaagh! Don't. No. No. Please don't."

He takes his finger from the trigger of the chainsaw and approaches cautiously.

"Oh, no, please. Don't saw me in half."

A man has his head buried in Mrs Tiggiwinkle's pinafore and is shaking and sobbing in terror. "I'll put you in my next film. I'll make you a star. Just please don't cut me into pieces..."

Cedric lowers his chainsaw and stares in disbelief. At first, it seems as though the man has his head on back to front. Then Cedric realizes that it's just his hair - his hair is back to front. The rest of him is normal. Fairly normal, anyway.

Cedric takes out his torch and shines it on the man's face. Across his forehead, holding his hair on the wrong way round, is a large sticker saying, Kiss Me Quick.

Cedric decides not to accept the invitation. He peers again at the face, blinking in the torchlight. It looks like Humphrey Head. "Is that you, Humphrey? It's Cedric here. Cedric Robinson. Hello there."

Humphrey covers his eyes as he cowers and trembles. On hearing Cedric's voice, however, he looks up. Suddenly, his face relaxes with a flash of recognition. "Oh, Cedric!" He stops sobbing, then leaps forwards and throws his arms round Cedric's neck. Cedric winces as his cheeks are drowned in kisses from the famous slobbery lips. "Cedric darling, how absolutely super to see you!"

Humphrey clings to the guide like a rubber suction pad. "Oh, Cedric I'm so grateful. I thought I was going to drown. Whatever can I do to thank you?"

Cedric tries to push Humphrey politely away and points out the tractor.

"Look, if you could just climb up on the trailer there, I'll take you back home in a minute. I've just got to saw this hedgehog in half before the tide comes in."

Each footstep is heavier than the last. They keep wanting to hesitate, to stop, to turn round, go back. The hardest thing is to keep clambering forwards into the sinking sands.

"Do you think we'll make it?"

No one answers. They're saving their energy, saving their breath, but as the tide comes in and the sands squelch more and more, the reality is there. They've made a terrible mistake. The tide is rushing in much faster than they can walk. They aren't likely to reach the other side.

"Just keep going."

Arnold and Warton stagger through the squelching sand with the dead weight of Kent Wilkinson slouched between them. His arms rest across their shoulders, weighing them down like an iron cape.

When Arnold had seen Kent fall face downwards into the rising channel, he'd tried to think of something amusing to say. Something clever. The boys had never known a situation so bad that they couldn't come up with a joke. But now, Arnold's brain doesn't seem to be functioning. He knows the time for jokes is over; other things are more important - heaving Kent out of the sands, staying upright, breathing, staying alive.

Spurred on by the whirring sound ahead, the three of them lumber towards the strange figure, still standing motionless in the sand. Sometimes the sound had echoed like the puttering engine of a tractor, then they thought they could hear a whirring like the hovering of a rescue helicopter. It hadn't seemed far away. But now, every step takes so much effort. The tide is rising, their shoulders are bowed with the extra weight, they are shivering with cold and rapidly reaching exhaustion.

Thirty

With great difficulty, Humphrey clambers inside the trailer. He huddles, shivering in the corner with his hands in his pockets and his coat collar turned up. "Tomorrow lunchtime," he tells himself. "Tomorrow, I shall be back in the wine bar. I shall be eating real food. I'll be warm and dry. I shall have returned to civilization and all this will be just a distant nightmare." He shivers. "Unless I've caught pneumonia and have to spend the rest of the summer in hospital."

"Back to the sands! Back into the shifting sands!"

Humphrey looks around. At first, he cannot see anything at all. The voice sounds like a disembodied ghost echoing out of the mist.

"Throw it back in the shifting sands. Throw the evil sign away."

He looks again and sees a figure, standing in the moonlight. It seems to be an old tramp, a woman dressed in old-fashioned boots and an ancient raincoat. She has long, straggly hair and a sack across her shoulder.

Humphrey stares open-mouthed. It looks like a phantom, an evil spirit, floating across the bay. The woman raises her hand as though she intends to point at him and cast some fiendish spell, but then instead she reaches back her arm. She's about to throw something at him. It looks like a small rock. Humphrey ducks as the missile comes whizzing through the air and lands at the other side of the trailer.

"Phhew! Good job that didn't hit me."

He slides down the trailer to try and make himself invisible. "Perhaps I'm hallucinating," he thinks. "Perhaps so many terrible experiences in one week have thrown my mind out of balance." He reaches for his brandy flask. He knows it's empty, as it was the last time he opened it and the time before, but there's always the hope that there might be one last drop of brandy in the corner somewhere.

The flask is definitely empty.

Humphrey glances over his shoulder and sees the eerie figure hobbling across the sands towards him. "If I cast that woman in a film," he thinks, "people would say that she was overacting." He shakes his head in disbelief. "Perhaps I ought to give up documentaries and try horror films instead. Hurry up, Cedric. Please let us get out of here alive."

"Let's put him down a minute."

"We can't. He'll sink."

"Come on, Kent. Try and walk."

Kent starts to regain consciousness as Arnold rubs his hand and massages life back into his face.

"Come on, Kent. Move your feet."

Kent takes a short gasp then, as they reach a small patch of drier sand, he manages to drag his feet along, painfully and slowly.

"Come on. That's it. We'll get there."

As they stagger forward, the figure in front becomes more distinct.

They had assumed it would be a man - a coastguard or a fisherman or even Bernard or Doctor Lune - someone who cared enough to come and look for them.

As they limp nearer to the figure, they realize that, whatever it is, it probably isn't a man after all. Perhaps it isn't even human. They begin to walk more slowly, uncertain now of whether to approach. Because what they see or what they think they see is so improbable that they can hardly believe their own eyes.

It appears to be much larger than a normal human being and it seems to be covered in hair. Perhaps it's some kind of abominable snowman. An enormous hairy monster with a long and slightly-uplifted, pointed nose, But the monster is wearing clothes - women's clothes and, what is most terrifying of all, she has a head filled with metal spikes, spikes which shine and glisten in the moonlight.

Kent stops for a second and rubs his eyes. But the figure doesn't go away.

When he first fell down in the sand, he felt certain he would never get up again. Then, when first he opened his eyes, he suddenly remembered stories of the Greek underworld, nightmare settings where evil men were forced to spend eternity performing horrific, never-ending tasks. And this surely must be one of them. His own personal concept of hell. Stumbling across the quicksands, struggling to keep himself from falling and heading towards an enormous hairy monster with spikes sprouting out of her head.

The boys stand still for a second, uncertain what to do.

Just then they see another figure and begin to feel faint with terror.

The sound that has been keeping their spirits alive is not a helicopter. It isn't anyone who's come to rescue them. It's a man with a chainsaw. Standing next to the enormous hairy woman is a big strong man with a chainsaw and he's slicing her in half.

"Aaaaaaaaagh!"

Kent screams.

The man looks up. As he sees the three boys standing and staring at him in a stupor his eyes widen and gleam. He abandons the hairy monster as the top part of her body begins to topple over. He lurches towards Kent, holding his chainsaw out in front of him.

"Aaaaaaaaaah!"

Kent tries to run, but he stands transfixed. The sands once again are gripping firmly on his feet

"Aaaaaaaaaah!"

And with every second, the homicidal maniac comes looming towards him with his chainsaw, as the head of his last victim finally topples forwards into the sands.

For the second time in half an hour, Kent begins to lose consciousness. But this time he is fainting with terror.

Thirty One

We drive further up the coast and I keep a look-out all the time for any signs of movement in the bay. Surely they must have taken torches with them? No one could be so stupid that they'd plan such a walk at night without even taking a torch.

I watch out for figures in the moonlight or tiny specks of torchlight but everything seems hopeless. I wish I could have today again. I wish I could have another chance.

Suddenly, I see something that looks like a pair of headlights, shining out in the bay. I don't see how it can be. "I think there's a light," I tell Sergeant Whiting. "I think I can see something."

The policeman stops the car and we climb out and have a look. At first, there seems to be nothing there, but then we see the two tiny specks of light, like parallel torches bumping across the sand together. They do look like a pair of headlights. They look like a car, driving across the sands back to the shore.

"It's a long way off," says the Sergeant, "but I think it's heading this way."

All I want is for the three boys still to be alive.

I listen. There's hardly any wind now and there isn't any traffic on the road.

"It sounds like a tractor to me." says Sergeant Whiting. "I think it could be Cedric Robinson."

We stand and wait as the lights bounce nearer and nearer. There's a tiny glimmer of hope inside me that Cedric might have rescued the three boys, but I try to smother it down. I don't want to be disappointed. You don't get disappointed if you never hope for too much.

"I think it is Cedric."

It does sound like a tractor and, as it comes nearer, there seems to be something behind it. I think it's pulling something. A tractor and a trailer. My hopes rise like a rocket because I can see a bunch of shapes. There's definitely something inside the trailer at the back. Please let it be people, I keep thinking. I can't help myself. Please let it be people. Please let it be Kent and Warton and Arnold and please let them be all right.

The tractor winds its way up off the beach. I still can't see inside the trailer. I only know that it's not empty. The driver steers up a track that seems to lead towards the road, then he disappears from view behind the hedgerows.

"I think it must be Cedric Robinson," Sergeant Whiting says again.

I just hope he's right.

There's a sudden putter of sound and the tractor belches into view. The second policeman steps into the road to flag down the driver. As he pulls up, we shine the torch on his face. He's a rosy-cheeked man wearing a big fisherman's jumper and a cap.

"Hello there, Cedric."

"Good evening, Sergeant."

I dash round to the trailer at the back to see what or who's inside and, when I look, I can't believe my eyes.

I just stand and gape.

Sitting in the trailer nearest to me is a very strange man, or it could be a woman, who seems to have his hair on back to front. The policeman follows me with his torch and I notice that the man - I think perhaps it is a man after all - has a sticker on his face which says Kiss

197

me Quick. I shake my head in disbelief. In the middle of the trailer is a giant hedgehog, sliced off at the waist. She's wearing a white apron. Her paws are outstretched in front of her, with little claws on the end. On the floor of the trailer, her head is lying, staring at the stars. She has sharp spines poking through her white frilly bonnet. I stand and stare, totally speechless.

"Hello, Jenny."

The voice comes from behind the hedgehog. I walk around the trailer and see Arnold, Kent and Warton. I never thought I would feel so pleased to see them.

"Are you all right?" I ask them.

They don't look all right at all. They're pale and shivering, crouched underneath a bright orange fisherman's jacket. I think it must belong to Cedric Robinson. Kent is holding something in his hand. When he sees me, he holds it up and shows me. It's the gold watch, I'm sure it is. The John Wilkinson watch.

There's a thousand questions I want to ask, but the only important thing at the moment seems to be getting everyone home and dry.

"We'll take the lads back in the car," Sergeant Whiting says. "Come on. They'll be suffering from exposure."

We help them down from the trailer and squash them into the back of the police car. I take off my coat and pass it to Warton, who's shivering uncontrollably and then I take off my jumper as well and give him that. I'm only wearing a T-shirt underneath, but it doesn't matter. The policemen give them their jackets as well. The boys seems to be in a state of shock, but at least they're alive. I think they've got Cedric Robinson to thank for that.

Thirty Two

DANGER
BEWARE
fast-moving tides
quicksands
hidden channels
In emergency phone 999 and ask for coastguard

I stand on the edge of the beach with my bird book and my new binoculars and watch the beginnings of the sunset. When I come for my walk in the early evening, everything is still. The red sun is reflected in the pools of water on the sand and they glisten with all the colours of the rainbow.

I often think about the mad woman, the one who stole Kent Wilkinson's watch, because, you see, she completely vanished afterwards. We never found out what happened to her. What was so strange about it was that no one in the village knew her; in fact no one could remember seeing her before. And you don't come across that many two hundred year old gypsies hobbling across the beach at night with skateboards under their arms. You'd think people would have remembered her. You'd think that, if people had seen her, they wouldn't have forgotten her in a hurry.

At first it seemed as though Humphrey Head might get the blame.

When Cedric tipped the semi-conscious lager louts into the back of his trailer, there was Humphrey sitting on the floor, dangling the gold watch in front of him as if he was trying to hypnotize himself. No sane person would have believed his story that an old woman had just hobbled across the beach and bowled the gold watch at him as he was nursing his empty brandy flask and praying to be telekinesthetized straight back home to Finsbury Park.

But the police believed him because his story matched what we told them about the mad woman coming to the house and ranting about throwing the Wilkinson watch into the quicksands. I told the police that I thought I'd seen her in the churchyard, but if she wasn't a local resident - and she certainly didn't look like a tourist - I can't think who she could be.

The boys were all right afterwards. They were shaken and upset and I don't think they'll be making any more treks across the sands at night. The school wasn't impressed with Dr Lune and Marjorie. "If it had been a state school," Penny said afterwards, "they'd have been dismissed for gross incompetency. With a place like that, they'll probably hush it up."

"Well, they were very keen on bird-watching," I mentioned.

"Bird-watching, my Aunt Fanny! Dr Lune noticed a heron down by the side of the pond and he invited Marjorie out with him to come and see the ostrich!"

A few weeks later, Bernard asked to see me in his office.

"Well, Jenny, you've been working here about six months now," he said to me. "How do you feel about it?"

I must have looked a bit puzzled. "About what?" I asked him.

"About the job. I mean, do you want to stay with us, or what?"

It seemed such a stupid question. Castle Head was the only place where I'd ever felt really happy. How could they imagine that I wouldn't want to stay?

"I, er...I've enjoyed it very much," I told him.

"Haven't you any complaints then?"

"Well, I didn't care for the Belmount boys."

"Ha." He grinned. "Well, I don't think they'll be coming any more."

"The work's been a bit hard sometimes," I told Bernard, "but I've got used to it now."

"Good, I'm glad to hear it. So, what kind of things do you prefer to do, Jenny? I mean, do you prefer working in the kitchen or looking after the children or what...?"

"I like the little children," I explained, "but most of all I like the animals. I enjoy looking after the baby goats and lambs and everything on the farm."

"Mmmm. " Bernard chewed his pencil and thought for a moment. "What about getting up early to feed them and going round late at night?"

"I don't mind."

"Mmmm." I hoped he was going to let me stay on.

"Well, if you would like to stay, perhaps we could arrange it so that you spend most of your time on the farm. Would you prefer that?"

I just nodded.

"Well, you see, there are all kinds of things to learn. You could learn to drive the tractor, you could learn about different diseases the animals get and different ways of feeding them. And there's lots of scope for expansion. We could get some more livestock if you wanted. We could buy some hens and chickens or perhaps some ducks and geese..."

I could hardly believe it. A proper job on a farm! I wanted to throw my arms round Bernard's neck and hug him. I didn't of course. I sat politely, smiling and nodding.

"I was thinking, you see, you could perhaps take special responsibility for the little children then - things to do with the farm, I mean, teaching them things. You could make up worksheets for them with different questions on and you could explain to them about how the lambs are born...you know, things like that..."

And look after the ducks and the geese and the hens and the goats. It sounded wonderful. "I'd really like to do that," I told him. "It would be lovely. I'd really like that."

"Right." Bernard looked pleased with himself. "Well, if we give you a proper contract, Jenny, and then, well, you'll have to have a wage increase as well of course. I'll come back to you later with that, when I've worked out what we can afford."

A nicer job and extra wages! "Thank you very much."

"You seem to have fitted in very well. Haven't you been homesick?"

I nodded. "I was at first, but then, well, I just feel as though this is my family now. That's what I've wanted..."

"Well, we're very pleased to have you with us, Jenny. Very pleased indeed."

I came here looking for my family, my real family, my proper mother. I don't know whether I've found out anything about her or not. She might be one of the descendants of Anne Lewis or she might not. It doesn't matter any more. I just want this to be my family now, here at Castle Head.

You see, the problem with having a proper family is

that you don't have any choice about who they are. You might not even like them. I could spend ages trying to find my proper mum then, if I met her, I could find that we don't get on at all.

And, of course, I know now that it isn't what family you come from that matters anyway. It's who you are that counts. If you're a nice person, perhaps you can go round making families for yourself anywhere you go, not by having babies, but by getting close to people.

I take out my binoculars and I focus on the redshanks and the oystercatchers. I bought my binoculars from a second-hand shop the last time I went back to see my mum. It was my first treat for myself with my new pay rise.

I've also been to the second-hand book shop in Carnforth and bought books about animal husbandry and how to look after ducks and chickens. I think some ducks would be nice on the pond in the farmyard. The children would like some ducks. And I've started to drive the tractor.

I put my binoculars and bird book away and then set off walking back through the fields. The quicksands and the fast-moving tides are all behind me now; I set off home for tea at Castle Head.

The Pit

ANN CHEETHAM

The summer has hardly begun when Oliver Wright is plunged into a terrifying darkness. Gripped by fear when workman Ted Hoskins is reduced to a quivering child at a demolition site, Oliver believes something of immense power has been disturbed. But what?

Caught between two worlds – the confused present and the tragic past – Oliver is forced to let events take over.

£1.95 □

Nightmare Park

LINDA HOY

A highly original and atmospheric thriller set around a huge modern theme park, a theme park where teenagers suddenly start to disappear . . .

£1.95 □

ARMADA

Run With the Hare

LINDA NEWBERY

A sensitive and authentic novel exploring the workings of an animal rights group, through the eyes of Elaine, a sixth-form pupil. Elaine becomes involved with the group through her more forceful friend Kate, and soon becomes involved with Mark, an Adult Education student and one of the more sophisticated members of the group. Elaine finds herself painting slogans and sabotaging a fox hunt. Then she and her friends uncover a dog fighting ring – and things turn very nasty.

£1.95 ☐

Hairline Cracks

JOHN ROBERT TAYLOR

A gritty, tense and fast-paced story of kidnapping, fraud and cover ups. Sam Lydney's mother knows too much. She's realized that a public inquiry into the safety of a nuclear power station has been rigged. Now she's disappeared and Sam's sure she has been kidnapped, he can trust no one except his resourceful friend Mo, and together they are determined to uncover the crooks' operation and, more importantly, find Sam's mother.

£1.95 ☐

ARMADA

RUN

WITH
THE
HARE

LINDA NEWBERY

Elaine has to decide whether to run with the hare or hunt with the hounds – is she really committed to Animal Rights or is she more interested in Mark?

"It is a genuine novel, setting its interests within a satisfying context of teenage relationships and activities. The book is a good story, an intelligent argument . . ."   *The Times Literary Supplement*

"Elaine is an intelligent and sensible heroine and by setting the romance in the world of Animal Rights, the author focuses attention on the adult world which appears confusing and often unfeelingly harsh to young people."   *The School Librarian*

Stevie Day
Series

JACQUELINE WILSON

Supersleuth	£2.25	☐
Lonely Hearts	£2.25	☐
Rat Race	£2.25	☐
Vampire	£2.25	☐

An original new series featuring an unlikely but irresistible heroine – fourteen-year-old Stevie Day, a small skinny feminist who has a good eye for detail which, combined with a wild imagination, helps her solve mysteries.

"Jacqueline Wilson is a skilful writer, readers of ten and over will find the (Stevie Day) books good, light-hearted entertainment."

Children's Books December 1987

"Sparky Stevie" *T.E.S. January 1988*

ARMADA

All these books are available at your local bookshop or newsagent, or can be ordered from the publisher. To order direct from the publishers just tick the title you want and fill in the form below:

Name _____

Address _____

_____

Send to: Collins Childrens Cash Sales
          PO Box 11
          Falmouth
          Cornwall
          TR10 9EN

Please enclose a cheque or postal order or debit my Visa/ Access –

  Credit card no:

  Expiry date:

  Signature:

– to the value of the cover price plus:

UK: 60p for the first book, 25p for the second book, plus 15p per copy for each additional book ordered to a maximum charge of £1.90.

BFPO: 60p for the first book, 25p for the second book plus 15p per copy for the next 7 books, thereafter 9p per book.

Overseas and Eire: £1.25 for the first book, 75p for the second book. Thereafter 28p per book.

Armada reserve the right to show new retail prices on covers which may differ from those previously advertised in the text or elswhere.

ARMADA